To Susan,
Enjoy!!
Dee Hartmann

Home, Sweet Funeral Home

by Delonda Hartmann

Home Sweet Funeral Home

LCCN: 99-91245

ISBN: 1-57579-172-2

Printed in United States of America

This book is dedicated to my granddaughters:
Abby, who inspired it, and Kat, who corrected it.

Thanks to Mark Frame of Parson Mortuary
and his wife Melinda for their invaluable assistance,
and to Joyce, Cindy and Vickie who said, "Yes!"

About the Author

Dee Hartmann, as an author, has had articles in *Guideposts* and *Financial Freedom Report*. She has been a theater reviewer for the *Muncie Star Press*, co-author of four plays, including *Bells, The Musical,* a play about teachers; *Middletown Unmasked* and *Middletown Divided,* plays about Muncie, IN; and *We Were Younger Then*. Dee is a member of Lambda Iota Tau, English Honorary; Phi Delta Kappa, Education Honorary; Women in Communications, National League of American Pen Women and American Association of University Women.

Dee is not only an author, but also a speaker. She has served as keynote speaker, commencement speaker, and seminar leader. She presents the challenges and failures of life in a humorous, informative way, enjoyed by young and old alike. Dee started college at age 39 against almost impossible odds. She was graduated (summa cum laude) in just 23 months. Her inspiring story is both funny and touching. She has a deep concern for people, for self-respect, for goal setting, and for the need to respect others. She has been a licensed auctioneer, a school-bus driver, a secretary, a waitress, a speech coach, a drama advisor, junior class sponsor, and a cheerleader sponsor. She has sold Mary Kay cosmetics, World Book Encyclopedias and lectured for Weight Watchers for three years, before she was defrocked. Dee taught at Blue River Valley High School and Ball State University where she worked on her Ph.D. She has spoken in 153 schools in Indiana and in 31 other states.

CHAPTER ONE

"This tire has been slashed!" I heard Matt mutter something that would get him grounded at home.

"What's wrong?" I couldn't see around him.

"We've got a flat. That's what's wrong."

I looked at my brother's pale face. "Who would do that?" I asked stupidly.

He shook his head. "I don't know."

"Have you ticked anyone off?"

He glared at me, his natural expression. "No, Leigh! I'm telling you I don't have a clue."

Now it was "we." Matt bought his precious Nova last fall from Horace Jacobs. Matt said the only reason he got such a great buy was because Horace was leaving for the Navy and had to sell. Great buy - a car painted red in back and green in front. A mobile Christmas tree. Now it was "We have a flat." That meant he expected me to help fix it. Mom wouldn't let either one of us get our license until we could check the oil and change a tire. I just never expected to.

After we got the spare out, I helped Matt flip off the hubcap. He folded his skinny 6'3" and squatted down, took the lug wrench and tried to loosen the lug nuts. "Are these welded on?" he growled, sweat popping out all over his face.

I'm not stupid, I kept quiet until he got the nuts loose. Then I helped him pull the tire off and get the spare on. Then he threw the tire in the trunk and we climbed in the car.

We sat quite a while without saying anything. Except for a few of the teachers' cars, the lot was empty.

I looked in the back seat. "Anything missing?"

He shook his head. Mr. Neatmik himself.

"I don't think so. I can't remember if I had my jacket or not."

"What are we going to do?" I asked.

Matt shrugged. "I don't know. If we tell Mom she'll go postal. Probably ground me from driving until I leave for college." He gave me one of those searching looks I hate. "Have you got any ideas? Anything strange going on that you know about?"

My face reddened. I hate that so much. "I had a couple of really weird phone calls last night while you were out with Kirby."

"Weird? How?"

"I don't know. Some guy called for Mike, but he wouldn't leave his name, and he kept calling back. He sounded scary."

"How scary?"

"Oh, you know, deep and gruff and kind of like he was trying to disguise his voice."

Matt narrowed his eyes. "What did you do?"

"I called Mom and Mike at Gran's and Mike told me to put the funeral home line on call forwarding. I was going to ask him at breakfast if the guy called back, but I forgot."

"That's it?"

I glared back. "Well, it's the only strange thing I can think of right now."

Matt rubbed the wheel with his right hand. "So, you don't think it was some joker?

I shook my head. "This was no kid. The man who called sounded fierce and grown up. Molly and I were watching a video in my room when the calls came. I didn't tell her I was scared, but whoever the guy was, he sounded like he could slash a tire. I just can't figure out why he would want to."

He started the car and put it in gear. "Me either. Maybe it was somebody who isn't going to graduate—you know, someone really mad at the school."

I nodded. "Yeah. Or maybe it was somebody who hates ugly cars."

Chapter Two

Cars filled the funeral home parking lot. Matt parked behind the privacy fence in back of the family quarters where nobody could see the Nova. We let ourselves in the back door and headed for the kitchen. Matt pulled out the peanut butter while I got the sweet pickles out of the refrigerator. Havoc came over and watched us with those big brown begging eyes. A German shepherd shouldn't like peanut butter and sweet pickle sandwiches. It's just wrong.

Of course, Matt made a little one for Havoc, who sat obediently until Matt gave him permission to eat.

Matt grinned. "Taking him to obedience school was the smartest thing I ever did."

"Yeah. He really trained you right."

We sat down in the den. Matt looked at the cover over Jed's cage. Covering up the parrot was the only way to keep him quiet. "Calling or a funeral?" Matt asked.

"Visitation for Mabel Franklin."

He nodded. "I forgot. Is the funeral tomorrow?"

"At 2:00."

He finished his sandwich and gulped down his milk. "Anybody else in?"

I sighed. "I hope not. I'm supposed to have a slumber party here tomorrow night. If I cancel again I might as well hang it up. The girls will really be pissed off."

"Nice bunch of friends."

I glared at him. "You know what I mean. The last two parties I planned had to be cancelled because we got bodies in."

He started upstairs to his room; Havoc padded along behind him, looking for all the world like a big silver and black wolf.

"Hey, Matt, aren't you going over to Kirby's this afternoon?"

He turned and tried to sound casual. "No. I don't think so. I want to wait until we find out whether that guy called Mike. The one that spooked you last night."

"You're worried, aren't you?"

He gave me one of his superior I'm-your-big-brother looks. "No, of course not. I just think something weird is going on, that's all."

That's all. After almost eight years I thought I was used to living in a funeral home. I knew the rules: answer the business phone politely; don't make noise during visitations; cover Jed's cage so he wouldn't screech when there are people in the funeral home, park the Nova behind the family quarters; be respectful in the chapel at all times. Then, there was my personal favorite - keep the fan on and the air purifier if you cook, and never cook anything smelly.

Mike's biggest rule: remember that no matter how many families we may have served, this is the first time these people have ever lost their mother. Mom's was "Don't be afraid. The living are more dangerous than the dead."

Right. Now something weird was going on. That's all.

Chapter Three

I went in the downstairs bathroom and washed up. Maybe if I pulled my hair back and refastened the clip it might tame the curls that kept popping loose. Maybe get the whole mop cut off like Molly did. Not. No sense wishing I had a smooth dark cap like hers instead of looking like a demented Kate Winslet.

We had stuff in the fridge to make a salad and there was some ham and cheese for sandwiches. While I set the table I thought about how Molly would sneer at me for making dinner. Molly says I'm *a good girl*, only she says it like that makes me stupid. I hate when she does that, but I can't tell Mom because she wouldn't let us hang if she knew. When I talked to Matt, he got real quiet for a minute, then he said, "So, do you want to be bad so Molly won't make fun of you?"

Rotten question. How to explain? "I don't want to be bad, but I don't want Molly to tease me when I try to do something nice."

Matt shrugged. "Maybe down deep inside she respects you for being good, but she doesn't want to admit it."

Yeah. Maybe. My brother, genius psychologist.

Anyway, I try to help Mom when I can, and I don't tell Molly. Helping out is only fair. After Dad dumped us and married Janet, Mom took a job at Ellis and Pearson Funeral Home to support Matt and me. A little kid in third grade, I made some kind of dinner when I got home from school, and tried to help Mom.

She was very cool after that first couple of weeks when she cried all the time. She even made it sound like an adventure when we had to sell the house on Wildwood Lane and move into an apartment. "Just think, kids, you'll be closer to school and to the library and to all the stores downtown."

"Sure thing," Matt mumbled. "And we can haul our bikes up two flights of stairs and chain them to a pipe in the hall so no one will steal them."

So, maybe everything wasn't perfect. The apartment wasn't great, but I thought our lives were pretty good until Mom decided to marry her boss, Michael Pearson. I really hated the idea of moving into a funeral home. So did Matt.

Mom tried to charm us. She and Mike took us out to dinner, to movies, to the zoo, to the Children's Museum in Indianapolis. The truth is, we really did like Mike okay. He was a big grizzly bear, only kind and real easy going, not much like our strict, skinny dad. Matt didn't say what he thought, but I kept thinking that it would be a lot harder for Mom and Dad to get back together if both of them were married to someone else. That's what I wanted more than anything, to have my family back

Then Dad and Janet adopted a baby. When Dad called he said it was so he and Janet could "share a child of their own." Great. Now they had Janet's son Roger living with them and a new baby girl. Not much chance of ever getting our Dad back. That's when we quit fighting Mom over Mike.

Now things were pretty cool most of the time. Dad and Janet moved to Florida, so we hardly ever saw him. We made Janet nervous, so we didn't go down to visit after one summer. At first we missed Dad, but pretty soon it was just a sore place that hurt if I touched it too hard. The pictures of Dad and us when we were kids got stuck into a box and put on a top shelf in my closet.

The family quarters at the funeral home were big, so both Matt and I had our own bedrooms upstairs, and our own TV's. We each had an extension of the family phone. Big deal. We both wanted our own lines.

The day of the flat, after Matt went upstairs, I waited for Mom to come and eat. Tomorrow was Saturday, I could do my homework then. I watched a little TV and called Molly.

Chapter Four

Molly sounded serious. "That's real scary about the tire. Did you tell your step-dad?"

"Not yet. He's at the calling for Mabel Franklin. Matt will tell him at dinner."

There was a long pause. I knew what was coming, but I didn't know how to stop it. Molly said, "I don't know why you're such a witch about Trevor Lewis."

"Yes, you do."

"You think he's just out for what he can get." Her voice was cold. "That isn't fair, Leigh. You don't know him."

"I don't know any of the big jocks at school," I said. "I just know his reputation."

"Well, I've cheered at all his games, and Trevor is a real sweetie."

"I just don't want you to get hurt." It sounded lame.

"Don't worry about me. I can take care of myself." Small pause. "I'll talk to you later." And she hung up.

Listening to the dial tone made me want to cry. It seemed like the more I tried to warn Molly about Trevor Lewis, the more determined she was to go out with him. Trouble was a magnet to her, and I couldn't do anything about it.

Probably the thing I hated most was having Molly mad at me. We were in the same day care; we started Johnson Elementary together, so we had been friends forever. There were lots of girls at school that she and I hung with, kind of our crew, but Molly was my very best friend in the world. We were the same height, same coloring, almost the same dark hair, except mine was curly. I kind of hunched over because of my boobs, but Molly just dared the world to look. Except for that, we looked like sisters, and we laughed a lot.

Trevor Lewis was a major creep, no matter what Molly's hormones were telling her. He flirted with all the girls, always touching, little pats here and little pats there, like girls were puppies. He had this real blond hair and big shiny teeth and dimples so deep that he looked like he should be on The Young and the Restless. He gave new meaning to trouble and that made him irresistible to Molly.

She cheered at all his games as if he was the only one on the floor. At first it didn't bother me much because all the cheerleaders were crazy about him and Molly was only a sophomore. But a couple of weeks ago he broke up with Tiffany Taggart again, and his roaming eyes fell on my best friend. I could die. If I did, I was in the right place. Home, sweet funeral home

CHAPTER FIVE

When Mom and Mike came in to eat, I was still brooding and still didn't have any answers. Matt came down with Havoc and we sat down at the table, very quiet.

Finally, I asked Mike. "Did that guy ever call back last night? The one that kept calling here while you were at Gran's?"

Mike frowned. "Yes, he called. Very strange, too. Sounded like he was trying to disguise his voice. He told me to forget the body in Florida, then he hung up."

Matt grinned. "There must be a lot of bodies in Florida."

Mom smacked him on the arm.

"What did he mean?" I asked.

"He didn't say. Just hung up. But this morning I got a call from Gertrude Hamilton about her grandson who died in Florida. She wants us to handle all the arrangements."

Matt and I exchanged glances. Gertrude Hamilton. Power Lady. Her husband owned the biggest bank in town and a couple of apartment houses and a lot of other real estate. When he died she got it all. The Hamiltons were big wheels in the country club and all the civic groups in town.

"I didn't know she had a grandson," I said. "I didn't think she had any children at all."

"His name is Larry Novak—Jillian Hamilton's son. He drowned in Florida. Apparently a friend of Mrs. Hamilton saw an article in the paper about a drowning which identified the victim as Lorenzo Novak of Chicago. She remembered that was the same name as Mrs. Hamilton's grandson." Mike paused. "What's really strange is that I called the embalming-shipping service to have the body shipped here, and they refused."

Matt and I both looked shocked.

"They refused?" I couldn't believe it.

"The man said they were shipping the body to Chicago in a Ziegler Box, and the arrangements had already been made."

"A Ziegler Box?" Matt asked.

"That's what they use when a body can't be embalmed for one reason or another. Novak's body had been in the water for at least two weeks and couldn't be embalmed, so they're shipping him in a Ziegler. It's a sealed metal box, screwed shut and put inside a regular casket."

"Why are they sending his body to Chicago?" I asked.

"Why were they sending him to Chicago?" Mike corrected. "I guess it's one of those ugly divorce things. Jillian married a Novak from Chicago, had this boy and then divorced his father."

"But the father got custody?" Mom asked. "That's strange, Mike. I can't imagine Jillian Hamilton giving up her child."

"I don't know any more than I've told you," Mike said. "It's one of those things nobody talks about, especially not around Gertrude Hamilton. Seems as if Jillian left Novak and then went out west. I haven't seen her for years."

"Did you know her?" I asked.

"She was a couple of grades behind me, but I knew who she was."

Mom smiled. "She used to date my bother Joe."

"Are you kidding? Uncle Joe dated Jillian Hamilton?"

"They even went to prom together. Remind me and I'll have Gran show you their prom pictures. They were a gorgeous couple. She used to come to our house a lot."

"What happened?" I love romances, even ancient ones.

"Oh, I don't know. Lots of things. Jillian wanted to be in the theater. She went to New York first, then to Chicago with an acting company. Joe went to college. They lost touch with one another. It happens."

I nodded. Just like The Young and the Restless. "Do you think Uncle Joe still loves her?"

Mom laughed out loud. "Of course not. He and Jillian were a high school romance that ended twenty years ago."

Yeah, sure. I bet Uncle Joe thinks about her all the time.

Mike rubbed his head as if it ached, then turned to Mom. "Frankly, I've put off telling Mrs. Hamilton the shipping service refused to send the body here. I told her everything would be all right, and then this jerk in Miami says they're sending the body to Chicago, period."

"Well, hey, Mike," Matt said, "maybe his father wants the body in Chicago for burial in the family plot or something."

"No. The father is dead, and Jillian wanted her mother to take care of the arrangements so that her son could be buried here in the family mausoleum."

"What are you going to do?" I asked, feeling a little chill.

"I've already called the sheriff and the state police. They said they would get in touch with the Florida State Police and see what could be done. This is the first time in twenty five years in the funeral business that anyone flat out refused to ship a body even after I offered to fax the papers. I don't like it."

Mom looked real uncomfortable. "I hate coincidences, Mike. I think it seems a little too neat that the man called about a body in Florida just before Gertrude Hamilton called you, and then the shipping company refused to ship the body."

And just before Matt's tire got slashed, I thought.

Chapter Six

Mabel Franklin's funeral was scheduled for 2:00 on Saturday. Matt and I had to be at school at 9:00 for commencement rehearsal. I put my saxophone in its case and sat down for breakfast. I gave Matt a look that asked if he had told Mom about the tire. The glare I got back translated into a big NO.

Mike started to say something about Larry Novak, but right then Jed began to screech and we all moaned and stopped trying to talk. What's the use? Even though Jed could sing and talk and do imitations, his favorite trick was screeching. His voice practically peeled wallpaper when he really got going.

"Jed!!" we all yelled. It didn't help.

Matt didn't talk on the way to school, but I could see by the way his hands were tight on the steering wheel that he was upset. I was sure of it when he parked The Nova as close to the front doors as he could get.

Walking into the building I saw Molly get out of her mom's Mercedes and start toward me. My heart gave one of those funny bumps. "Hi." I tried to sound normal.

"Hi," she said, not stopping. I walked along with her.

"Is your mom coming back to get you, or do you want Matt to take you home?"

She smiled at me, one of those empty smiles that means less than nothing. "No, I don't think so. Trevor is going to take me out after practice. We're going on a picnic."

My throat tightened so I could hardly spit it out. "That's nice." It was not what I wanted to say. Maybe she could tell.

"And I think he and I may be going to the movies tonight." Her voice was as bright as her smile.

"What about my party?"

She kept smiling. "I hate to miss it, but you know how it is."

I nodded and walked faster. I didn't want to walk with her, the traitor. Sure, I wanted to say, I know how it is. You're willing to dump your best friend for a big fat jerk who'll make a fool out of you.

I never knew you could play a saxophone with your stomach hurting like that, but I did it. Molly stood in back of the band next to the drums holding her mallet ready. I only looked back at her once. She was flirting with Andy Hudson, best drummer in Sparta High School. I used to think that she played the bells so sweetly they sounded like angel chimes. Now every time I heard that little ching it made my head ache.

The seniors stomped in, acting like idiots until Mr. Shmidt finally yelled at them. Finally we played Pomp and Circumstance again and they marched in some kind of order and took their seats on the gym floor.

What a bunch of creeps. I hated them all, including Matt. Big, handsome Trevor Lewis, basketball star, major trouble maker, kept smirking. I wanted to see if his big head would fit into the bell of my sax.

After practice Matt got his cap and gown and we walked out to the car. "Does Molly want a ride?"

I shook my head no.

The Nova looked okay, no flats. I was surprised when Matt unlocked his door. "Did you lock the car?" I asked.

"Did you see me unlock it?"

I glared at him. "I thought you were just testing the key to see if it worked. I've never seen you lock it before."

He opened the door, unlocked the passenger side, put his cap and gown in the back. "Whoever cut the tire took my old jacket," he said gruffly. "Get in and let's go home."

"Right, Prince Charming."

We rode for half a mile in silence. Finally, I couldn't stand it. "So what's your deal? Why would anyone want that ratty old jacket?"

He grunted. "I don't know. The whole thing has me freaked out. We could have been out of there an hour ago if the great god Trev hadn't been showing off."

I felt my throat tighten. "He's taking Molly out on a picnic today."

He made a low growl. "Big trouble."

"I know," I whispered. "I know."

Chapter Seven

We found everything upside down at home. Mom was frantic - she couldn't find Jed. We had to be quiet because of the funeral. That meant we couldn't go around calling the bird at the top of our lungs, the way we wanted to. Instead we went from room to room, checking closets and the tops of things, calling softly, "Jed. Jed. Jed."

"How did he get out?" Matt asked.

Mom shook her head. "I don't know." Her eyes were red. "I came in from the office right after the funeral started. I thought I heard something at the back of the house. So, I went back to see if someone had come around out of curiosity. I found Jed's cage open and empty."

People must really be fascinated by funeral homes because sometimes they come around back to the family quarters, probably to check things out. They're usually disappointed when they find the privacy fence. It's six feet high, made of wooden slats, and it keeps the backyard private for cookouts without the whole world watching. Havoc is loose back there, so very few people come through the gate when they see the sign BEWARE OF THE DOG. Sometimes people open the gate anyway; then Havoc growls and shows them his long white fangs, and they close the gate real fast.

Matt frowned, "Didn't Havoc bark?"

Matt named Havoc after a line in Julius Caesar. "Cry havoc, and let slip the dogs of war,'" Matt quoted. "Isn't that great? It's a promise of how fierce this pup will be someday."

I remember how we all laughed because while Matt picked the fiercest name he could think of, the puppy kept licking his hand and trying to kiss his face.

Mom shook her head. "No, he didn't. I never even thought about it, but he didn't make a sound."

Matt hurried outside. We heard him yell, "Mom!! Mom!! Come here quick!"

Mom and I ran outside to find Matt kneeling next to Havoc who was moaning and drooling. Matt looked up at us with tears in his eyes. Havoc wouldn't even try to stand up, but he kept raising his head to look at Matt.

Mom hurried back in to the telephone to call Dr. Andrews, our family veterinarian. She ran back where we were kneeling by Havoc. "Hurry," she said. "Pick him up. Doc's going to meet us at the office."

We hurried. Matt and I wrestled Havoc up in our arms and carried him to Mom's van. She drove very fast. Matt kept rubbing the fur behind Havoc's ears.

"You'll be okay. You'll be okay," he whispered.

I thought my heart would break.

We pulled up into the NO PARKING zone. Doc stood waiting on the sidewalk. She has taken care of Havoc since we first got him, has given him all his shots, recommended the obedience school Matt took him to. She loves Havoc almost as much as we do. She took him out of Matt's arms and hurried inside.

In the waiting room Mom and I sat huddled together, trying not to cry out loud. Next to us Matt sat very still, but tears kept running down his face, and his hands never stopped rubbing the sides of his jeans. We all sat close together, not looking at the chart of all the breeds of dogs on the wall across from our bench. We tried not to think about what might be going on in the examination room.

When she came out to see us, Doc was very serious, which scared me even more. "Maggie," she said, looking at Mom with something more than worry, "someone poisoned Havoc. He vomited a small piece of steak. Luckily he didn't eat much of it, probably because he's so well trained. It saved his life."

"Poisoned?" Mom was dumbstruck. "who on earth would poison Havoc? He stays in our back yard, doesn't bother anyone. Donna, this is crazy."

Matt shook his head. "Havoc isn't supposed to take food from anyone except us."

Doc frowned. "Did you find any of your clothes near him?"

"No," Matt started to say.

"Yes," I blurted. "I saw your jacket right next to where we found him. The one that was in your car at school. I didn't think anything about it."

Doc nodded. "That would do it. Whoever poisoned Havoc probably wrapped the steak in your jacket to make him think it was from you."

"And Jed is gone, too," I said, not looking at Matt's white face.

"Jed? How did he get out?"

Mom shook her head. "I don't know."

Doc looked stern. "Do you think someone let him out on purpose? Maybe the same person who poisoned Havoc? I don't like the sound of this Maggie. What's going on at your house?"

Chapter Eight

Mom rubbed her eyes. "I don't know, Donna. I just don't know."

Doc patted Mom on the arm. "You'll have to leave Havoc here. Tonight at least. But there's no sense in you staying." She put her arm on Matt's shoulder and said gently, "I'll call you as soon as I know anything."

Matt's face told us how hard it was for him to leave his dog.

All three of us were quiet on the way home until I said, "Mom, someone slashed the tire on Matt's car yesterday at school."

Mom frowned. "Slashed it?"

Matt nodded. "It looked deliberate."

Mom's frown deepened. "What's going on, kids? I just don't understand."

"All this started with that call the other night," I said suddenly.

"You mean about Larry Novak?" Matt asked.

"Sure. Why else would someone slash Matt's tire unless it was meant as a warning of some kind? Why let Jed out? Why poison Havoc? It's all tied together somehow."

Mom shook her head. "I think you're right, Leigh. But it doesn't make any sense. I need to talk to Mike." We were close to the funeral home and had to wait for the procession to pass before we could turn in. All the cars followed the police car and the silver gray coach, little flags snapping in the wind.

The house seemed really quiet without Jed. Matt looked lost without Havoc. When Mom started getting stuff out of the refrigerator I must have looked puzzled.

"It's for your slumber party tonight."

I leaned against the counter. I had forgotten the party. I swallowed hard. "Do you want me to cancel it, Mom? I mean, with all the stuff that's going on. You know."

She started making sandwiches, putting boiled ham on slices of white bread, cheese on whole wheat. Finally, she said, "Leigh, you know what it's like to be in the funeral business. If we call off the party when there isn't a body in, everyone will speculate. That's bad enough. But if word gets out about the tire, about Havoc, and parents don't think their daughters are safe at a party here...well, we might as well close the doors."

She saw the expression on my face. I was ready to cry.

"Honey, this isn't your fault. Your friends love to come here for parties because it's a funeral home. They feel safe being scared, just like at a spooky movie. It would be different if there was any real danger. Understand?"

I nodded, miserable. Then I shook myself and started helping get out chips, dips and cookies. The party I dreamed about all year was turning into a nightmare.

Chapter Nine

Matt came in while we were working, looking like forty miles of bad road. "Do you think it would be okay if I call Doc?"

Mom nodded.

He came back into the kitchen a few minutes later. "Doc says he's holding on. She thinks he'll be okay." He gave a weak grin. "I can pick him up tomorrow."

Like an idiot I burst into tears.

When Mike came into the kitchen, he found all three of us hanging onto each other, Mom and me crying hard.

"What's going on?" he asked.

We pulled apart and Mom and I reached for tissues while Matt told him about Havoc. I told him about the tire.

We stared at one another. Finally, Mike said, "Can you think of anyone who would do anything like this?" He sounded calm, as usual, but I could tell he was upset because he was jiggling the change in his pocket.

"Leigh thinks it's all tied in with Larry Novak," Mom said.

Mike nodded. "That's the obvious choice. Anyone else?"

I had to say it. "What about Old Man Modrine?"

Everyone thought about it. Old Man Modrine lived alone across the street to the south, and certainly seemed to hate the funeral home and us. He was the last of the Modrines who founded the town and named it after themselves. Sometimes when he didn't appear for a couple of weeks, we wondered if he was dead. Then he'd come charging out of his house in his old baggy clothes. He'd work for a while in the jungle that passed for a front yard, then disappear again. In the summer the tall shrubs and weeds hid the lower part of his house completely. In the winter we could see the peeling paint on the porch and the windows. The house was the same sad gray as old tombstones. Only the faded red bricks looked good, at least from a distance. We didn't go up close to look, because everyone said Old Man Modrine shot at trespassers.

The front doors of the funeral home faced the front of his house, which seemed to really upset the old guy. When he had one of his temporary fits of insanity, he'd come over and scream at Mike about the traffic. Then he would stomp back across the street and disappear inside the Modrine Mansion. There were stories about the secret passages and hidden tunnels in the house.

"Maybe he hates dogs," I said, lamely. "You know, he's got those mangy cats that he lets out at night. Maybe he wanted to keep Havoc from barking."

Matt shook his head. "Everybody knows Old Man Modrine is nuts, but Havoc hardly ever barks unless someone is trying to get into the fence, and I don't think he could hear him clear over to his house. Besides, I can't see the old guy sneaking over to school to slash my tire."

Neither could I, but I couldn't imagine anyone else doing it either.

Mom pushed her hair back off her forehead like she does when she's worrying. "What about Casey Grubbs?"

Mike looked at her, surprised at the question. "Grubbs? Why?"

"Well," Mom said, "he's been so belligerent on the telephone lately. His funeral home hasn't had much business for the past two years, and I know he resents us. He hates doing so much charity work."

Mike shrugged. "I do a lot of charity work, too."

"I know you do, but there's a big difference, Mike. That's almost all Casey gets these days. You do it because you have a commitment to the funeral business."

I remembered one time when the county brought in a vagrant found dead in the park near the lake. Mike put a suit on him, and had a minister come in to conduct a funeral service. He said, "This is what we do here."

Mike looked annoyed. "It's Casey's own fault that his business is down He drinks. He lets the grounds grow up so his place looks abandoned. He doesn't keep his coach or the family car washed. The inside of his building smells musty and it doesn't look clean. Of course, people who can afford to go somewhere else don't take their loved ones there."

It sounded like an old argument to me. Mike was really hot about keeping the funeral home clean and pleasant. He had a big aquarium in the lounge because he said fish were soothing. All the pictures on the wall were peaceful landscapes. Besides keeping the place clean, the grounds were full of flowers, thanks to Willy.

Great minds must really think alike. Matt said, "Willy's been acting pretty wacko lately."

Mike almost smiled. "Willy's always been a little strange, for twenty years."

"I know," Mom said, "but you remember last week when you told him he had cut the bushes too low. He was really angry. He told me he was going to quit and he was going to make Marie quit too. She blames it on his medication."

I shivered. Willy had been so nice when Matt and Mom and I first came to the funeral home to live. He used to let me ride the mower with him, or watch him work in the flowers, or let me help wash the cars. I thought he was great then, but he hadn't been much fun lately.

Mike looked around at us. "I don't know. I'd hate to think Willy would poison Havoc."

Matt nodded, "Or go to the school to slit my tire."

Mike looked tired. "Any other ideas besides Clarence Modrine, Casey Grubbs or Willy?"

We shook our heads.

"It could be one of them, but I still think it's all got something to do with Larry Novak," I said.

Mike nodded. "So do I, Leigh. The state police called and they're going to meet me at the airport tonight to pick up the body. The Florida state police barely stopped the shipping company from sending it to Chicago, so they have an officer there to supervise the shipment to me."

Mom looked worried. "That sounds very serious, Mike."

"I know. Harold is going to go over to the airport with me. Frankly, I don't know if this is going to be the end of our problems, or the beginning."

Chapter Ten

I didn't feel real comforted that Harold, the deputy sheriff who made Barney Fife look like a genius, was going with Mike to the airport. I wondered if he was even allowed to carry a bullet in his pocket, but I didn't say anything. Mike and Harold had been friends for years.

"So," I asked, scared of the answer, "is my party still on?"

"What party?" Mike asked, not smiling.

"Leigh has a slumber party planned for tonight," Mom said. "She had to cancel the last two she planned. I'd hate for her to do it again, especially when we don't have a body in."

Mike shook his head. "Maggie, this isn't the time for a party. Too many things aren't right around here. Jed's gone, Havoc's at the vet's, someone cut Matt's tire. I'm not sure this is a good idea. Maybe the girls could go to your mother's."

I wanted to throw up. The girls would hate going to Gran's. I would hate going to Gran's. We might as well not even have a party.

Mom smiled at him. It was her charming smile, and it usually worked. "Mother is willing to come over here and help me. That makes two adults. The girls are bringing their CD players and sleeping bags so they can sleep in the chapel. It's always such a big treat for them to scare themselves to death." She paused, then brightened. "Why don't you ask Harold if the sheriff's department would patrol this evening. Tell them you're going to Indianapolis and there's a bunch of teenage girls staying overnight. Just say you'd feel safer. What do you think?"

He looked at her and then smiled back. Then he turned to me. "This is really a big deal for you, kid?"

I nodded.

Mike sighed. "Okay. I'll call. But, Maggie, I'm counting on you to keep track of the girls. Don't let them go prowling through Roselawn the way they did at the last party."

"I promise," Mom said. Then she gave me the not-so-charming, I'm-your-Mother-so-listen-to-me look. "No cemetery games tonight."

"No way. We'll stay in, eat a lot, watch some videos, and talk. Okay?"

"Promise?"

I nodded. Anything. "I promise."

"Okay."

I asked myself, What can go wrong? Later I wondered why anyone would ask themselves such a stupid question.

Chapter Eleven

I thought Mike was finished, but he sat tapping his fingers on the table. "Maggie, did you see the three strangers who came to the funeral today?"

Mom didn't hesitate a second. "They didn't seem to be part of the Franklin family, and I don't think they looked like anyone from around here."

Matt grinned. "Maybe aliens?"

Mom frowned at him. "Very funny. They were big city people. Their suits must have cost a small fortune, and they kept looking around all during the service."

Mike wasn't smiling either. "Did you notice anything else?"

Mom thought for a minute. "I was looking at them, and when they saw me watching them, they eyed me until I turned away. Most people would be embarrassed and turn around and at least pretend to listen, but they didn't. If it was a contest, I lost."

Mike rubbed his hand over his eyes. "I should have told you before, but I didn't want to worry you."

"What?" Mom's voice was shrill. "What should you have told me?"

"I'm pretty sure Larry Novak's father was in the mob in Chicago."

"The Mob? Like the Mafia?" Mom asked.

"Drugs. Prostitution. Gambling. Gun running. You name it."

Matt and I exchanged glances. It sounded like a television movie. Jillian Hamilton in I Married the Mob. Wow.

"How do you know?" Mom asked. "Did Gertrude Hamilton tell you that?"

"Not exactly. She kept avoiding the subject of her former son-in-law. Finally, I guess she got tired of my questions because she gave me a scathing look and said he had been involved in some 'unsavory activities' with a group of 'most unsuitable companions' and had 'lost his life through violence.' I decided to change the subject."

Mom shook her head like she was trying to deny the whole idea at first. But then she said, "I bet that's right. Joe told me something about the Novaks years ago, right after Jillian got married."

Poor Uncle Joe. I bet his heart was broken when she got married to someone else.

Matt wasn't thinking about love. "Maybe those three guys you saw at the funeral were hit men."

"Don't be ridiculous," Mom said, but she looked more scared than angry. "You've been watching too much television."

We sat looking at one another, wondering what we had all gotten into, something that wasn't a TV show.

Chapter Twelve

I went up to change my clothes and think about things. It's a great bedroom with big windows all across one wall, two big window seats. Too bad the view was Roselawn Cemetery. I plopped down on the nearest window seat and watched some guy on a riding mower go up and down the rows between the tombstones.

The party had seemed like such a good idea. Most of the girls had summer camps to go to for journalism, or cheerleading, or church or something, so we wouldn't all be able to get together again until school started. By then Hilary Ashton would be gone. Her family was moving to Ohio the last week in June because her dad got transferred. So, this party was our last chance. Last chance. Made me have goosebumps.

Molly was supposed to come over early to help me get ready. Now that was out. Melissa had a couple of new CD's. Amy was bringing her portable CD player. Holly was coming, Jennifer, Stephanie, Lisa, Carrie and Hilary. We called ourselves the Terrific Ten. So, tonight we could be the Nervous Nine.

At the last party we tied helium balloons on all the chairs in the east chapel, on the casket biers and the flower stands. We had a seance that scared us all to death. Everyone loved it. Only the last time there wasn't anything to be afraid of.

Now Jed, our early warning system, had disappeared. He always screeched like mad if a stranger came around. Havoc always protected the back yard, and now he was gone, too. I thought about the strangers at Mabel Franklin's funeral and felt like a hand was on my throat.

Then I looked at Roselawn. The mower was gone, but I saw a man walking down the gravel paths that twisted between the small weathered tombstones. He kept looking over at the funeral home. He paused by one of the tall monuments that stood at the crossroads of the paths, and looked up at my window. He leaned back against the base of the monument and stared up as if he knew I was there, like he wanted me to see him watching. The huge stone tilted at a crazy angle, the base sunken more on one side that the other. On top, one angel: raised hand beckoning. The hand at my throat tightened.

I meant to tell Mom when I got downstairs, but just then Mike came in from the office. "I talked to Harold, and he's going to have his deputies drive past during the evening. Police Chief Williams said he would have a half-hour patrol until tomorrow morning."

Mom nodded. "Good."

"There's one other thing. Come here and let me show you something I'd forgotten was here until the chief reminded me." Mike led us into the reception area by the front door. On the wall by the coat rack was a small wooden plaque that I'd seen at least a trillion times in the past eight years. I just never noticed it before. It said Ellis Brothers Mortuary…June 10, 1910.

Mike pushed the plaque to one side. Under it we could see a recess with a lever inside.

"Hey!" I said. "I never knew that was there."

Mike looked at the lever, which was red and a little rusty looking. "It's an alarm the Ellis brothers had installed. It's hooked up to the police station. According to the chief, no one's ever used it in his memory. He wants me to pull it to see if it still works." He reached into the recess and pulled the lever down.

Nothing happened. We just looked at one another for a minute and then Mom giggled. It startled Mike at first, and then he started laughing. That got us all going. I think I laughed too long and too hard and I wanted to cry at the same time.

Just then the telephone on the reception room wall rang. Mike answered it. "Okay. Sure. Right. That's great."

He hung up and turned to us, still grinning. "It works." He reached into the recess and pushed the lever back up. "After all this time, it still works. That's amazing."

Surely," Mom said, "that hasn't been here since 1910."

"No. I don't think so. Probably thirty years, though. The Ellis brothers got really paranoid as they got older. The Chief said that they often called to report a prowler who usually turned out to be the mail carrier. So, I guess they put this extra alarm in so they would feel safer."

Mom shook her head. "Mike, we've got silent alarms on every door and window in the place. This extra thing seems silly to me." She looked at the plaque and grinned.

Mike agreed. "It doesn't hurt anything to know that it's there."

I thought of the Ellis brothers getting more paranoid as the years passed. I think I can understand that.

Chapter Thirteen

Before my friends arrived, Gran came over. She brought her latest novel to read, an overnight bag packed with hair stuff and lotions and creams, and a black leather emergency pouch she always took on trips. When I was little she let me check out the pouch with the little bottles of rescue remedy, arnica oil for sprains, peppermint oil for indigestion, Tei-fu for muscle strains, band aids, and antiseptic handy wipes. She had a pocket knife, emery boards, a magnet, eye drops and aspirin. I loved it.

Gran was funny most of the time, and pretty cool. She had her own real estate business and stayed busy with her work and her charities. Mom said she needed an appointment to see her. Gran just laughed. She laughed a lot, but when Mom made her sit down and told her everything that had happened, I saw her face change.

"This is serious, Maggie," she said.

"I know, Mother, I know," Mom said, a little impatient.

"Listen to me. If these men you saw today are gangsters, we could all be in danger here. I can't imagine they would be intimidated by a bunch of screaming teenagers."

She smiled at me so my feelings wouldn't be hurt. They weren't. The girls do scream a lot. I remembered the time we were having a party in the chapel and Jennifer passed around peeled grapes and said they were dead men's eyeballs. Carrie almost fainted that time. But she screamed really loud first.

"Well," Mom said, "what would you have me do? Do you want me to bring all of the girls over to your house?"

Gran laughed, but I tightened, afraid she might think that was a good idea.

Mom spread her hands out in a surrender gesture. "I obviously can't tell their parents when they bring the girls here that we're all in danger and they should take their children home. That's what I would like to do, but you know what would happen if I did."

Grand nodded. "The story would be all over town in about eleven minutes."

Matt came into the kitchen where we were talking and stuck his two cents in. "Try five minutes, Gran. Modern mothers have cell phones."

We all smiled a little, but only on the outside. Mom and Gran were right. If we told anyone that the funeral home might be a dangerous place, the story would spread like wildfire.

Mom paced. "If people begin to believe they aren't safe here, we might as well lock the doors and forget about ever being able to serve the families around here."

CHAPTER FOURTEEN

Mom pinched the bridge of her nose the way she does when she's worried. "If I really thought there was any danger, I'd just lock all the doors and send the girls home, but we don't really know." She stopped in front of the refrigerator and glared at it.

"Speaking of locking the doors..." Gran said cheerfully.

"Right," Mom sighed, "Let's be sure all the doors are locked."

I moaned a little. Eleven outside doors and a million windows. Even with silent alarms on them, they had to be locked every night. Usually Mike took care of it. Guess who got to do it tonight.

"Leigh," Mom said, "you go ahead of us and turn on the lights."

I nodded.

We started walking around checking each door. I left the lights on and for once no one said anything about the cost of electricity.

The big double doors on the west side had to open wide enough to allow caskets to be carried out to the coach by the pallbearers. The deadbolt was locked. Great name.

Matt checked the locks on the windows as we went from room to room.

The front door by the office was locked tight. That was the part of the original mansion that the Ellis brothers had turned into the funeral home. We could see out through the old leaded glass to the circle drive. Through the glass everything looked as if it were under water, warped and slightly discolored. I wondered if that was the way the outside world looked to the angel fish in the 20-gallon aquarium in the lounge.

The second set of leaded glass doors opened into the vestibule outside of the formal chapel. Locked too. Big enough to let a casket through, I thought again.

The six-foot doors in the formal chapel were secure. By this time my back felt stiff from holding my breath. Every room was familiar to me, but suddenly it all seemed strange, sinister.

Mom went through the preparation room to check the outside door, the one Mike used to bring in bodies for embalming. None of us went with her. We'd all been in there before because Mike didn't want us to be afraid of the prep room. There wasn't much to see, a super clean room with a steel table and stainless steel sinks. All the embalming equipment was kept in the cabinets. Mom walked across the tile floor, heels clicking at each step. I kept repeating to myself, "It's just another room. That's all."

Three more outside doors in the garage, plus four overhead doors. We walked through the garage listening to the echo of our whispers, past the coach, the ugly brown van used to deliver flowers after funerals, the big black Cadillac family car, and good old Nova. Mike had moved Matt's car inside when he took the smaller van to go after Larry Novak's body.

"Look inside the vehicles," Gran said softly.

Mom gave her a look. Then she went over and tried the doors on all four to see if they were locked. She peeked in to see if anyone might be hiding inside. No one. I tried not to think of what we'd do if anyone was.

The outside doors were locked. Okay, so far. Except that next was the basement. Real fast I could name ten things I'd rather do than go down the basement, starting with geometry straight downhill to being locked in a room with Trevor Lewis.

"How many outside doors are there to the basement?" Gran asked in a cheerful voice that didn't fool anyone.

"Three," Mom said, not even trying to sound cheerful. She turned to me. "Do you want to wait up here, Leigh?"

I hate the basement. I nodded, relieved.

"Matt?"

"I'll go with you," he said, but his face was pale and I could see his jaw muscles were set.

I watched them start down the stairs. All three of them creeping, feeling each step before they put their weight on it. I felt guilty, letting them go alone. Big chicken. If anything was going to happen I wanted to be with them. We'll all go together when we go.

I crept down the stairs behind them, my heart banging with every step.

Gran turned around, saw me, and screamed.

I screamed.

Mom screamed.

Matt made some kind of strangled cry.

"Leigh Allison West!" Gran said, "You scared me to death!"

"Well, you didn't do me much good either, screaming like that!" We glared at one another for a second and then burst out laughing.

Mom pushed her hair back out of her eyes. "Do you suppose our nerves are a bit on edge?"

The truth is, I really was scared. Usually I was fine, even when there was a body in one of the chapels. After five years I knew that the dead don't move or come back. They didn't do any of the stupid things like in those dumb horror movies. Dead is dead. Period. But this was different. Someone alive was out there. Or inside.

The basement didn't smell musty and funny because fans made the air move around. It touched my face like ghostly fingers. The lights lit up the middle of the room and left the corners full of shadows.

Matt ran into one of the bulbs and started it swinging back and forth. The light scattered and the shadows seemed to move. I hurried to catch up with Mom and Gran.

The two of them marched across the basement without looking around. Their heels tapped, tapped, tapped as they walked, close to one another. I stayed right behind them, near enough to be able to smell Gran's Eternity perfume.

For a minute I wanted to run away, just like when Mom told me she and Mike were getting married. That day I had screamed at Matt, "I'd rather die than live in a funeral home."

Matt had glared back. "Well, then he'd get your body. How would you like that?"

I hit in him the chest as hard as I could with both my fists doubled up. I knocked him down. It hurt him , too, because he cried, and I was glad. Now, checking the basement brought it all back and I felt like I was ten again, not sixteen, almost a junior in high school, practically grown up.

The whole tour didn't take more than fifteen minutes, but it felt like hours. Gran wanted to check the second floor even though there were no outside doors there. "We need to be sure the windows are locked. It's just a feeling I have," she said, smiling.

Mom gave her a questioning look, but things were so weird that she decided to go along with it.

We checked the lounge. The angel fish were swimming in their bubbly world, the air pump making a little hum. The windows were closed and locked. In the selection room I remembered when my twin cousins Brad and Chad had hidden under the caskets, behind the skirts, the day of Grandmother Ethel's visitation. "The twins hid under the skirts," I whispered to Gran.

Mom heard me. "Leigh, honey, we're checking to make sure nobody can get in, not to be sure no one can get out."

Gran and I just looked at her. We didn't want anyone getting in or out.

Mom nodded. "Right. Let's look under the skirts."

No one was there.

"What about the attic?" Matt asked. I wanted to kill him.

Mom shook her head. "The attic is secure enough. There aren't any outside doors and the windows are too high for anyone to get in."

Just then the floor above us creaked. We all looked at one another. Mom reached out and locked the dead bolt on the hall door that led up to the attic from the funeral home side of the building. "Old houses creak," she said firmly.

We all nodded, but Matt wouldn't meet my eye. I thought I heard the sound of a footstep and I bet he did, too. But neither of us wanted to go up to check. Good thing.

Chapter Fifteen

A half an hour before the girls were due, the doorbell rang. Mom sighed, "They're starting early." Gran laughed.

I opened the door. It was Molly. We stared at one another for a few seconds, then she shrugged and gave a little laugh. "He didn't show up. Trevor. He was supposed to pick me up two hours ago."

I nodded. "So you decided to come to the party."

Her face tightened like she was ready to cry. "Don't you want me?"

I stepped back out of the doorway so she could come in. "Oh, shut up. Come on in." I didn't say I told you so. Gran always says that even if you did tell someone not to do something, reminding them is a bad idea. Either she remembers you told her and doesn't want to be reminded, or she forgot you told her and doesn't want to be reminded.

Molly picked up her duffel and a paper bag full of chips and pretzels and corn puffs. I looked at the stuff in the sack. "You didn't need to bring anything."

"Yes, I did." I saw the look on her face and nodded.

"Where is Havoc? He didn't bark when I came in the gate?"

I felt the tears burn my throat. I told her about finding him, about the trip to the vet's, with Havoc moaning and drooling all over Matt while we all cried. I told her about how worried we all were.

"Who would do a thing like that to a beautiful dog like Havoc?" she asked.

I shook my head. I didn't have an answer.

Molly looked ready to cry, maybe over Havoc, maybe not. "How is he now?"

I shook my head. "Matt keeps calling. He may be able to bring him home tomorrow." I decided to tell her the rest of the story. "Jed's gone, too."

Molly's eyes widened. "What...?"

"We don't know. His cage was open when Matt and I got home from rehearsal."

She whistled through her teeth, a sharp little sound. "This is super weird."

I nodded. "I know. And you can't tell anyone. The other girls won't even notice about Havoc or Jed, and you can't say anything. You know how funny people are about funeral homes. It's okay for us to tell scary stories, but real bad stuff is out."

She nodded slowly. "Dad always says his paintings would sell better if he were dead. It makes Mom furious. Last night she said she ought to kill him and set us up for life. I didn't think it was funny."

I had a little cold chill. "I don't think it's funny either."

Chapter Sixteen

Just then Amy and Melissa came in carrying a big bag of stuff.

"What have you got?" I asked.

"You'll see!" Amy laughed.

"It's a surprise!" Melissa grinned.

I had to smile back. The two of them were always coming up with something fun. Gran said that what one didn't think of the other did.

Hilary and Stephanie showed up right then, laughing like idiots over something. Mom asked Hilary if she was hungry and of course, she said yes. Hilary was always hungry, and skinny as a rail. It wasn't fair. She ate like a couple of horses and never gained an ounce. It would be easy to hate Hil for that except she was so funny and never teased anyone about being fat, especially Holly, who was very sensitive, and wasn't really fat at all, just chunky.

Mom gave Hil a glass of milk and two chocolate chip cookies. Mom loves to feed people; Hil loves to eat. Works out.

The rest of the gang came in about the same time: Jennifer, Carrie, Lisa and Holly. Everyone talked at once. Hil said, "You guys are making so much noise you could wake the dead."

Everyone laughed, even though she'd told that joke at every party I ever had.

Mom ordered pizzas for us, laid out potato chips, pretzels, corn chips and salsa, plus the stuff Molly brought. We filled paper plates and sat around the kitchen table, or in front of the fireplace in the living room. No food in the funeral home.

Matt built a fire and we flopped down on the floor and talked. I thought he was supposed to go over to Kirby Meyer's for the night, but he was sticking around. When the pizza came he piled his on a plate and went up to his room. Mom never said a word.

We ate like it was our last meal. What do you want on your tombstone?

Holly picked up a piece of pepperoni and put it in her mouth. "Mrs. Pearson, you may have to roll us into the chapel."

Mom smiled. It looked a little forced to me.

We all went into the east chapel where the girls had put their sleeping bags.

"Let's tell ghost stories," Jennifer whispered, rolling her eyes as if she were scared.

We all laughed. Jennifer wasn't afraid of the devil. Carrie was the baby of the bunch. She was afraid of everything and everybody. The last party Jennifer scared Carrie into hysterics. For a while I thought we'd have to call her dad to come to get her. Carrie was afraid of a lot of things, especially the funeral home. We finally kidded her out of being so upset, but Mom wasn't amused.

This time Carrie spoke up fast. "No. No ghost stories, Jen. You know how they scare me."

Jen smiled. "Okay. We'll take a vote. How many for ghost stories?"

Everyone yelled, "Yes. Yes. Yes." Everyone except Carrie and Hilary. I was surprised at Hil. She was usually the first one to vote for a seance or something scary.

"So," Jen said, "what are we going to do with our two scardy cats? Lock 'em in the closet?"

Everyone laughed, but it wasn't good laughing. We all knew Jen too well. Locking people in closets is a rotten idea, but it was a real Jen-thing. When we were in sixth grade she actually did stick a first grader into the janitor's closet at our grade school. She held the door shut until a teacher came along and caught her. She got into a lot of trouble that time.

Carrie's face turned white as snow, which excited Jen. Her eyes glittered. I took Carrie's arm and growled, "Leave her alone, Jen. Carrie and Hil can go in and watch TV with Mom and Gran. You guys get your sleeping bags fixed."

The girls grinned and took their sleeping bags to the south end of the big chapel where we usually put the casket when there is a viewing. They all thought that was the scariest place in the whole funeral home.

"This is really nice of you," I whispered to Hil as she and Carrie and I went into the family quarters.

She grinned at me. "Carrie is my friend."

Mom was in her bedroom sorting laundry. Gran was watching television and reading. Matt was back downstairs talking on the family phone. Can't tie up the business phone in the evening.

"Gran, do you care if Carrie and Hil watch TV with you while we tell ghost stories?"

Gran looked up from her book. "Of course not." She handed the remote to Hil and went back to her story. I looked at Matt. He grunted something I took to mean okay, and kept talking in a low voice

I went back to join the others. There were only six girls sitting in a circle: Jennifer, Holly, Stephanie, Lisa, Molly and me. "Where are Melissa and Amy?"

Jen shook her head. "Doing something mysterious with the bag of stuff they brought."

I had a cold chill. I wished I knew what they were doing.

"Are you ready?" Jen asked.

We nodded.

Chapter Seventeen

"Well," Jen began softly, "once upon a time..."

"When, exactly?" Holly asked, giggling.

"Who cares *exactly*?" Lisa laughed.

"Yeah. Yeah." Everyone agreed.

Jen gave Holly a look and went on, "As I was saying, once upon a time, in this very funeral home, a crazy old man died and his body was brought here."

Everyone shifted. Right here. In this very funeral home. A crazy old man. I thought of Old Man Modrine and shivered a little.

"Put out a couple of those lights," Jen ordered. She was on a roll now. Bossy. I jumped up and turned off two of the three lamps we had on in the chapel. The light from the remaining lamp made a circle around the table, and cast shadows on the rest of the room. Spooky enough.

"The crazy old man's family brought him here because they thought that he and old Claude Ellis were friends. But they weren't. The truth was that Claude Ellis and the crazy old man were bitter enemies and had been that way since they were kids."

"Why? Why were they enemies?" Stephanie asked.

"Because...well, because..." Jen paused, "because they had both been in love with the same girl when they were in high school, and she liked Claude the best."

"Claude was an old bachelor," I said, trying not to grin.

"Yes. Yes, that's right," Jen said. "He was. He never married because the only girl he ever loved...the one they both loved...died right after they graduated. She had...hmmm... she had the plague."

Everyone moaned, "Oh, how awful. How terrible."

I put my hand over my mouth. The plague, right.

"Anyway, neither one of the men could ever forget her. She was so beautiful, like a princess in a fairy tale. Her parents were rich and lived in a mansion right here in Modrine."

"Where? Where?"

Jen waved her hand. "Oh. It burned down years ago. Anyway, her family was very rich and because they knew that their beloved daughter had loved Claude Ellis best of anybody, they left him a lot of money when they died. That made the crazy old man even madder."

"What was his name?" Holly asked. Holly liked to have all the facts.

Jen narrowed her eyes, the way she does when she's going to say something really mean. Then she said, "Bruno. His name was Bruno. He was German. A Nazi."

That was good. None of knew much about Nazis except what we just read in lit class about the Holocaust. We all shivered a little.

"Anyway, Bruno was even more resentful and angry after Claude inherited all that money from Rebecca's parents."

"Rebecca," the girls whispered. We all liked that. Now we had names for all the major characters, Claude, Bruno and Rebecca.

"There were even people who said that Bruno used to go to the cemetery and talk to Rebecca's grave sometimes. Late at night, when the moon was full."

Better and better.

"Now, Claude didn't know that Bruno still loved Rebecca all these years, and he didn't now about Bruno going to the cemetery on the nights when the moon was full, but he did have a funny feeling every time he saw his old enemy."

"A premonition," Holly breathed softly.

"Exactly. A premonition," Jen agreed. "Sometimes when Claude would see Bruno he would feel a strange chill go down his spine. Then, he would laugh it off because he knew chills are silly things to believe in." Jen spoke in her most menacing voice. Chill bumps.

"So," she went on, deepening her voice and speaking more softly so we all had to move closer to hear her, "one day they came to tell Claude that Bruno had died, and since everyone except Claude and Bruno thought they were old friends, they wanted to bring the body here to Ellis Brothers Funeral Home."

It was getting to the good part. Pretty soon, when we were all leaning in to hear every word, Jen would scream real loud. It worked every time.

"They didn't have embalming in those days," Jen said, glaring at me in case I was going to contradict her. I just shrugged. She went on.

"So, they brought the body in and planned to bury it right away before it got all rotten."

"Oh," the girls moaned. They liked this.

"When Claude was arranging the body in the casket he thought he saw one of the eyes open."

"Ohhhh."

"So he felt for a pulse, but there wasn't one. Then he went and got a mirror and held it up to Bruno's nostrils to see if there would be a sign of breath."

We'd all seen that in a Dracula movie.

"There wasn't a sign of life."

Everyone was leaning forward now. Even me.

"They had the funeral that very day, and took poor old crazy Bruno to the cemetery to be buried in the family plot."

Everyone looked west toward the cemetery.

"Right over there," Jen whispered.

Shudder.

"Then," she said so softly that we could scarcely hear her, "that night when Claude had gone to bed, and was trying to sleep, he heard someone walking around in the funeral home."

Everyone looked around uneasily.

"AND GUESS WHO IT WAS?" Jen screamed.

We all screamed with her. Then we saw them. Two figures were walking toward us from the far end of the chapel. They were dressed in rags and their hair stood straight up on top of their heads. They looked like rotting corpses. Just like The Night of the Living Dead. Their arms hung straight down at their sides. Black sockets for eyes, absolutely white faces with green on their cheeks. White faces. Clown white. Like makeup. Melissa and Amy.

The girls were all screaming and scrambling over each other to try to get into the family quarters. Stephanie must have wet her pants because there was a dark stain spreading all over the seat of her jeans.

"Guys! Guys! Hey, wait!" I yelled. No one listened. They were all getting out of there, over, under, around or through. I heard yelping as people got stepped on.

Meanwhile Jen was holding herself, laughing so hard I thought she would explode. I hoped she would. This was way worse than the time she passed around the peeled grapes.

Melissa and Amy were laughing so hard they were crying. The tears washed the white makeup off in streaks down their faces.

I was watching them, getting ready to tell them off when I saw something move in the hall, cutting off the light from the wall lamp we keep burning all the time. Whatever it was cast a shadow through the doorway and into the chapel. My breath caught in my throat. For a minute I thought I was going to faint. Mike was gone. Matt was in the other room. There was someone else in the funeral home.

Chapter Eighteen

"Come on, you two," I said in what I hoped was a normal voice. Inside I felt as if some of my bones dissolve. I wanted to scream, or cry, or run, or all three at the same time, but I didn't dare because then the person in the hall would know I'd seen the shadow.

Melissa and Amy came across the chapel in slow motion. I wanted to yell at them to hurry. I bit my lip to keep myself quiet. They were both laughing like hyenas and hanging onto one another for dear life. Behind me Jen was holding her sides and bending over from laughing.

"Very funny," I said. "You guys have probably ruined any chance of ever having another party here for the rest of my entire lifetime."

"Oh, come on," Jen gasped. "It was a great joke. Don't be so square."

Right. At the moment I felt like a three-dimensional square, a cube. Maybe even an ice cube. I could hear hysterical howling from the family quarters.

"Mom is probably two degrees off boiling even as we speak."

Melissa giggled. That sent Jen and Amy off again.

"Just shut up," I said, "and let's go in and try to calm everyone down." Sure. We'll calm everyone down while a stranger prowls through the funeral home.

I had to tell Mom right away, but I didn't want to scare the girls any more than they already were. I headed for the family quarters, followed by Jen, Melissa and Amy, still cackling like geese and hanging onto one another.

That's when it hit me like a fist in the stomach. I couldn't tell Mom. I heard her say that if there were really any danger she would make the girls go home. I knew her. Even if it ruined the business, she would still do it.

Great. What if all I saw was just a shadow and there wasn't really a stranger in the funeral home after all? What if I had just let the story get to me? What if I was wrong?

I couldn't tell Mom. But I had to tell someone. The problems ran around in my head like a troop of circus clowns. Clowns with white faces and hollow eyes and painted tears. I hated clowns.

Could I tell Gran? No. She was another adult, like Mom, and adults always stick together. Besides, she might even go charging in to try to find out who was hiding in the funeral home. She wasn't afraid of anything.

Molly? Maybe I could tell Molly. She always understood things. But not this, not family business.

I had to tell Matt. He was the only logical person. Good old level-headed Matt. He would know what to do. But, what if it had been Matt, playing a trick on us? Maybe he had slipped in while Jen was telling her story.

We walked into the family quarters. Mom stood there, furious but controlled. I was hoping she would send the girls home. That would eliminate one problem. But no. She had that icy control that meant she was gearing up for a real let-'em-have-it , big-time lecture.

I looked across the room at Matt where he sat looking worried, not even listening to Mom's warm up. If Matt was the one who cast the shadow, he sure got back quick. For a second I wondered why couldn't Molly like him instead of Trevor? Matt looked close to handsome since he got contacts and had his braces off. No. There's something creepy about your best friend liking your brother.

I tried to signal him without doing something obvious that Mom or Gran would notice. With Mom busy winding up for her award-winning lecture to Jen and the girls, I could probably wave a flag at him and she wouldn't notice. Gran, on the other hand, was watching me. I could bet she would corner me the minute I tried to get Matt away alone.

"You girls know better than to behave like this," Mom was saying. "Look at Holly."

Clearly, Holly had fallen apart. She hung onto Hilary for dear life, tears still running down her cheeks. Molly didn't look too good either.

In the light Melissa and Amy looked stupid, not scary. Both of them had teased their hair into spikes and sprayed the messes into hard ridges all over their heads. They had used some kind of green hair spray that turned Melissa's red hair purple and Amy's blonde curls into green thorns. Tears from laughing had streaked their white makeup so it ran down onto their ragged clothes, leaving dark spots on their white shirts.

Mom looked at them for a minute without speaking. I thought she was going to chew them out big time, but she didn't. She shrugged as if she had reached the end of her rope and wasn't in the mood to tie a knot in it and hang on.

"You two go to Leigh's room and clean yourselves up. You'll need to shower a long time to get that goop out of your hair." She sighed. "Don't leave the bathroom in a mess, either."

Melissa murmured, "No, Mrs. Pearson." She grabbed Amy's hand and they started upstairs. Mom stopped them. "Wait until I find some old towels for you to use."

She went into the master bedroom. I heard Jen let out a long breath. She probably figured that Mom's fury had been defused. I wasn't too sure.

I looked over at Matt. He sat in the lounger, tilted back, with a funny look on his face. Maybe he was worried about Havoc. He didn't look at me. The television flashed and bleated some late movie that no one was watching.

Gran came over and put her hand on my shoulder. "Are you all right, Leigh?" she asked.

"I'm fine," I lied. "I just wish the girls hadn't gotten everyone so upset." A partial truth. "Was Matt in here watching TV the whole time?"

"Yes, why?"

"No reason. He said he might go out with Kirby tonight, that's all." It sounded dumb.

"He's been here the whole evening," she said, patting my back. Then she did the strangest thing. She went over to the door that led into the funeral home and locked the dead bolt. She turned around and saw me watching her and gave me a sickly grin.

"The sleeping bags are in there." It was Matt. He had come up behind me while I was watching Gran. "We'll have to go in and get them out."

I shuddered a little. "Yes."

Gran closed her eyes slowly and then opened them again. "Yes," she repeated softly. Why couldn't someone say No?

"Well, girls," she said loudly, "let's all go in the chapel and get the sleeping bags."

No one said a word. Then Holly whimpered. "I don't want to."

No one else spoke. They didn't move either.

"That's all the more reason for us to go in there right now and get the sleeping bags," Gran said brightly. "We'll get Melissa's and Amy's too, and you girls can take them upstairs to Leigh's room." She paused. "Or would you rather sleep in the guest room? If you would, I can sleep down here on the couch."

Just like Mom, giving us choices.

"Leigh's room. Leigh's room." Several of the girls spoke at once.

"Fine," Gran said. "Let's go then."

She unlocked the dead bolt and opened the door to the chapel. "Matt," she said firmly, "you turn on the rest the lamps."

He stalked in, disgusted with the girls. Maybe it was just as well I hadn't had a chance to talk to him. I'm not too sure how brave he would be if he knew.

I followed him in to gather my sleeping bag and Melissa's and Amy's while he turned on the lights. I remember how Mom always told me, "The living are more dangerous than the dead." Right. Whatever made the shadow at the end of the chapel hadn't been one of the Living Dead. It had been one of the living - period. And Mom was right. That was a much scarier idea.

The lights made the room look as comfortable as and pleasant as a parlor.Gran stood by the door ushering the girls through so that each one had to come in and get her sleeping bag. Stephanie followed me, with Jen right behind her. Lisa and Holly were hanging on to one another. Hilary came in to get her bag and Carrie's.

Everyone but Jen walked a little too fast. She picked up her bright red bag and turned to Gran. "It really was pretty funny," she grinned.

Gran smiled back at her so Jennifer wouldn't think she was angry with her. But, I know Gran, and she didn't mean that smile. I had seen her lock the door to the chapel. She was worried, too. "That's okay, Jennifer," Gran said. "But I think it will be more fun for all of you if you sleep in Leigh's room instead of in here. Her carpet's softer."

I looked away so Jen couldn't see my face. The carpet in the chapel is exactly like what's in my room.

When everyone went back into the family quarters, Matt started to turn the lights off for the night. "Don't!" I said. "Just leave them on tonight." He looked at me for a couple of seconds and then turned the big brass lamp at the north end of the chapel back on.

"Right," he said.

Gran watched us, but she didn't ask any questions.

Just then Matt called, "Hey, come here you two."

We hurried over to where he stood looking out the north windows at the Modrine Mansion across the street. Every light blazed. "What's going on over there?" Matt asked. "There must be a million lights on."

We could see lights on all over the main floor and upstairs, too. There was even a light in the third floor window.

Gran shook her head. "I've never seen the place lighted up before in my life."

Even as we watched the lights began to go off, one at a time. We watched for several minutes until the house hunched dark as usual.

Gran rubbed her neck like it was aching. "Strangeness keeps piling up, doesn't it?"

Matt and I both nodded. It sure did.

We went back into the family quarters, leaving lamps burning on two tables in the chapel. When we closed the door behind us, I saw Gran turn the dead bolt again.

"Maybe we should lock the other adjoining doors," I said, trying to sound casual, as if it was not a big deal. Just lock the doors, you know, for the heck of it.

Gran and Matt looked at me without saying a word, then Gran nodded. She left us standing by the door and went into the master bedroom. A door in there that hardly anybody knew about opened behind the drapes into the chapel. I didn't know if it even had a lock.

In the living room, the girls giggled and laughed like fools, holding their sleeping bags like teddy bears. I didn't think they were funny.

I heard Mom say, "Ready to go upstairs?"

"Yeah. Sure. Great." The girls trooped up the stairs dragging their stuff and laughing at how scared they'd been.

Gran came up behind me and rubbed my shoulders. "Very tense, little girl," she said softly.

I tried to grin at her, but my mouth felt like I'd had a shot of novocaine.

"Let's go lock the door to the garage," Gran said.

Mom was watching us. "Where are you going? Aren't you going upstairs with your guests?"

" In a minute," I said, and forced my stiff lips into something like a smile.

"Leigh is going with me and Matt to lock all the doors that adjoin the funeral home," Gran said in a voice that sounded as strained as my smile. "There's no problem, Maggie; we'd just feel better. That's all."

Mom looked at the three of us, narrowing her eyes a little. Then she said, "Okay. Let's lock the doors. Mike can ring the bell when he gets back with the body."

"I locked the one in your bedroom already," Gran said as Mom started toward her room. She turned and gave Gran another one of those speculating looks, but she didn't say anything.

We locked the door to the basement, then the door to the garage. Mom paused for a second, then turned the dead bolt. "Mike will understand. He wanted us to be careful."

When I started up the stairs I could hear the girls laughing in my room. I never enjoyed a party less in my life.

Two doors from the second floor led into the funeral home, and one went to the attic. The place used to be one of the major mansions in town, and it had more doors than a hotel. As I started to lock the door to the attic, the knob turned slightly just below my hand. I twisted the dead bolt fast.

I heard Matt take a deep breath behind me. He had seen the knob turn, too. My heart pounded. I turned and looked at him.

"Someone is in there," I whispered. "I saw a shadow downstairs. What are we going to do?"

He shook his head and swallowed hard. "I don't know, Leigh. I just don't know."

Chapter Nineteen

We looked at each other for a couple of seconds that seemed like hours. The knob did not turn again, but we knew what we had seen and we both knew that if we told Mom what was going on, she would clear out the house, and we could tell the funeral business good bye. Nobody takes their loved ones to a place where strangers prowl around at night.

"It's a good thing there are no bodies in right now," Matt said, as if he could read my mind.

"Mike's gone to get one," I reminded him.

"Yeah."

I looked at my tall gangly brother, acting as if he weren't one bit afraid. "We can't tell Mom," I said.

"I know."

"Besides," I said, trying to sound as brave as he was trying to make me think he was, "everything's locked now." I didn't fool him.

Matt frowned. "Do you think Gran would sleep in your room with you and your idiot friends?"

I wanted to be offended at the idiot part. "Why?"

He shrugged. "Maybe she could keep the girls from wandering around. Between Jen and your buddy Molly, there's not much they wouldn't try. Like sneaking into the funeral home after everyone goes to sleep."

I saw his point. Jen thinks rules are meant to be broken, and Molly isn't much better these days. "They couldn't get past Gran."

"That's the idea." He paused. "But you'll need to lock the door, too. There's an old skeleton key in my closet that works on my door. I bet it work on yours. Try to get Gran in there, get the idiots settled, and then you lock the door."

I must have looked skeptical. He patted my shoulder. "Hey, kid, there's a bathroom in there. No one needs to get out. And, besides, if you're careful, no one needs to know the door is locked."

"Do you think Gran will do it?" I asked just as she came up the stairs with her suitcase full of stuff.

"What are you two conspiring about out here?" she asked.

I grinned at her. "We were wondering if maybe you'd make a deal with us."

She set her bag down. "What kind of a deal?"

"We wondered if you'd be willing to sleep in the monkey cage tonight," Matt said.

"What?"

"He means would you sleep in my room tonight to be sure that none of the girls try any more stupid tricks. You could have my bed."

She watched me closely while I talked, her gray eyes way too shrewd behind her glasses. Then she turned to look at Matt, who was trying hard to look innocent.

"And you think I could keep the zoo under control?" she asked.

Matt and I nodded.

"Okay," she said. "I'll try. None of those girls needs to be out wandering around tonight. Mike's due back any minute from Indianapolis with Larry Novak's body. Your mom says Harold called the Indiana State Police and faxed the papers to them. They called the Florida State Police, who went to the shipping service and got the body shipped to us."

Mike had already told us all that, but Matt and I both acted as if it were news to us.

"Anyway, it's all very exciting. And to add to our little adventure, there's a big storm coming."

Of course, I thought. We have to have a storm to go with all this mystery. I thought of how much Havoc hated storms. Whenever lightning flashed he would dive for Matt's bed and tremble until after the thunder passed. I looked at Matt and knew he was thinking the same thing.

"I've got to go to Doc's office," he said, forgetting everything else. "Havoc can't be there alone in a storm."

Gran frowned, but I knew she was worried, too. "Matt, it's past midnight."

"I know, but I can't help it. Storms terrify Havoc. He's already sick. This could kill him, locked in a cage away from home. I have to go."

Gran didn't argue. She patted Matt on the arm. "Go down and talk to your mother. I'll go on into the monkey cage, and God help me."

She opened the door to my room where the girls were all at fever pitch laughing and playing CD's full blast. The door closed behind her, and suddenly the music stopped. Matt and I exchanged glances. Good old Gran.

He motioned me to follow him into his room. I walked behind him, with my nerves still jumping. We both saw the doorknob turn. Someone was downstairs and someone was in the attic, and neither one of us knew what to do.

Matt opened his closet, turned on the light and reached up to a small nail just above the top shelf. He took down a long, thin skeleton key and handed it to me. "I think this will work on your door, too. Don't let Gran see you lock it. She's hard to fool and she's already suspicious."

I nodded.

He turned off the light in the closet and closed the door. I followed him out of his room. He flipped the switch and closed his bedroom door. Neat freak.

"Want me to go down with you to talk to Mom?"

He looked at me, and I knew he didn't need a little sister. "Hey, Matt," I said, "it may take the two of us to convince Mom to let you go."

That did it. He nodded. "Come on, then."

It turned out that Mom understood right away when Matt said, "I've got to go over and stay with him. The storm could kill him."

She reached for the phone. "I'll call and have Doc meet you there." She forced a little smile. "She'll understand."

She hung up and turned to Matt. "She'll meet you in 20 minutes."

He turned away so she couldn't see the tears in his eyes, but not quite fast enough. I saw Mom's eyes fill too, and my throat hurt from holding back my own tears.

"Mike took the van, so you better take the family car. The windshield wipers aren't any good on the Nova, and with a storm coming..."

"Be careful," she said, handing Matt the gold key ring with two gold keys.

He took them gingerly. He had never driven the big black Cadillac before. It was the car Mike used to take families to the cemetery for funerals.

We walked to the garage. Mom unlocked the door and we went out into the cavern which echoed our footsteps like a giant drum. I stayed back at the door to the house, while mom walked Matt to the Cadillac. Once he was in the car, I pushed the button for the middle overhead door. He started the car, put it in reverse and backed out into the storm.

CHAPTER TWENTY

It was a good thing Mike hadn't let one of the staff take the family car for the night. Then Matt would have had to drive the coach. I almost giggled at the thought of him tooling up to Doc's in a long black hearse.

After Matt pulled out, I pushed the garage door opener and closed the overhead door. Mom came back to stand by me. We looked at the garage full of shadows that seemed to gather in the corners. I felt Mom shiver next to me. We hurried back into the house and locked the door behind us.

"Gran's sleeping in my room tonight," I said. I didn't want Mom to go up to check on her mother and find the guest room empty. That would tear it.

"Why?"

I knew she'd ask. "Well, hmmm, she thought it would keep the girls from wandering around the funeral home during the night. Especially Jen and Melissa and Amy." It was close to the truth. I didn't mention Molly.

"Good," Mom said. She hugged me. "You go on up to bed yourself. You'll be exhausted in the morning."

I looked at the dark circles under her eyes. "Are you going to wait up for Mike?"

She nodded.

I walked carefully up the stairs, keeping to the outsides of each step so they wouldn't creak. Even though the old house didn't make all the spooky sounds like in movies, the stairs moaned a little when you stepped in the middle.

At the top of the stairs I paused at the door to my room. I didn't hear any racket. The girls were probably pretty ticked about Gran staying in there with them, but I couldn't help it.

They'd have to get over it. Sometimes you have to do what you have to do.

As I reached for the door knob, the thought struck me; Mike was due back any time, but right then Mom was downstairs alone. I stood for a couple of seconds trying to decide what to do. Then I turned around and went back down the stairs to be sure Mom would be okay.

I walked into the kitchen just as Mom opened the refrigerator. She turned around and saw me, went white and staggered as if she were going to faint.

"Mom!!" I ran to her.

"Leigh," she gasped, "you scared me to death."

"I didn't mean to. Honestly, I didn't mean to. I just wanted to be sure you're all right."

She hugged me. We both cried. What an awful day it had been.

While we stood there hanging on to one another we heard someone call my name.

"Leeeee."

We stared at one another.. It came again.

"Leeeeeeee."

My stomach rolled, goosebumps jumped up on my arms and the little hairs on the back of my neck stood straight out. I felt my skin tighten all over my body, like it was creeping over my bones. The voice was the exact one Matt used to try to scare me in the basement, a strange, haunting, drawn-out call, like a lost soul. Only Matt was gone.

Mom's face had no color at all, just putty. We clung together. She was trembling too.

Then we heard a raucous wolf whistle. Then came the sexy call, "Hey, Baby. Baby. Baby. Baby."

Then a howl, like Havoc singing.

"Jed!" We said it at the same time.

We ran to the patio doors and looked out into the yard. We couldn't see anything in the trees, even with the security light on.

Mom opened the door. The wind tossed the trees and moaned a warning. The storm Gran had predicted was coming in fast.

"Jed. Jed." We called.

"Leeeee. Leeeee." Wolf whistle. "Hey, Baby. Baby. Hey, baby." Then another blood-curdling howl.

I started out onto the patio when suddenly he flew past me, through the patio doors and into the living room, straight through to the utility room and into his open cage.

Mom closed the patio doors and locked them, and we followed Jed, laughing hysterically. Crazy bird. Crazy, wonderful, stupid old bird. He sat on his perch flashing his red mask as he ruffled his bright green feathers and picked himself with his yellow beak. He screeched at us. It was the same horrible sound he always made, the one we hated. It sounded wonderful. We grinned at one another.

A noise in the garage sounded like the garage door opening. "Matt?" I wondered.

"Mike?" Mom asked.

We heard the garage door go down. We walked over to the inside door and stood there listening. We heard a creak like the back door of the van opening, followed by thumping. Then we heard the squeak of wheels as Mike wheeled the casket into the prep room. A long silence followed. We figured Mike was probably prying the crate open to check the Ziegler box with Larry Novak's remains.

Then we heard the door to the prep room being closed and locked. Footsteps. The doorknob turned. We waited. A key turned in the lock and the door opened to the sight of a serious Mike.

"I'm glad you locked the door," he said to Mom. They hugged each other as if he had been in China instead of Indianapolis.

Mom looked up at his tired face, and grinned at him. "Jed's back. Screech and all."

Suddenly, Mike looked ten years younger. He loved that stupid bird. He always talked to him as if Jed could understand every word. He's the one who taught Jed to say "Hey, Baby, Baby, Baby."

After we showed him the bird happily asleep under the quilt the covered his cage, I started to go back upstairs. Mike stopped me. "Leigh, did you see anything strange at the Modrine Mansion tonight?"

"Whoa. How did you know? There were lights all over the house. Then they all went off. It was weird."

"I heard about it on the CB coming back from Indianapolis. Apparently, Mr. Modrine reported hearing a prowler, and the police when over and checked out the house. They didn't find anyone, but things had been disturbed in the basement." He paused. "When I stopped at the sheriff's office they told me someone had been watching the funeral home out of the basement windows."

"How do they know that?" Mom and I asked at the same time.

"They found binoculars and some Polaroid pictures of the funeral home below the window. They must have scared whoever it was before he had time to grab his things."

I swallowed hard.

"I don't want to scare you, Leigh, but you need to stay alert and be sure to let me know if you see or hear anything out of the ordinary."

Right. Like maybe a stranger in the funeral home, and someone in the attic. I nodded but didn't say anything because I didn't trust my voice.

"I need to go up and tell Matt about all this," Mike said.

"You can't," Mom said. "He's gone to stay with Havoc. There's a storm coming."

Mike nodded. He understood.

Almost on cue lightning flashed through the windows, followed immediately by a crash of thunder.

"Close. That one was close," Mom whispered.

The next flash illuminated the room for a second. Then even before we heard the thunder, everything went dark, completely dark. The electricity was out.

Chapter Twenty One

Mike growled something that sounded like cuss words, which gave me a clue to how upset he was since he never cusses, or maybe only when the lights go out.

Standing frozen in the pitch dark room so we wouldn't run into anything, we could hear the hail hit the patio doors like vicious pebbles. Another flash of lightning and Mike opened the pantry door and reached for the kerosene lamp we kept for emergencies. A box of matches lay on the shelf next to the lamp, along with candles and holders.

Mike fumbled around until he got a match lit and got the lamp going. Then he went back into the pantry and brought out candles to light for me and Mom.

"You better go check on your friends," Mike said. "There's another lamp filled with kerosene and some matches in the closet in the west guest room. Light that and put it in your room until the power comes back on. I'll get the flashlights from the garage."

I nodded. All those girls up there in the dark meant trouble.

I walked carefully up the stairs, keeping my left hand up to block wind from blowing out the candle. The flickering light made shadows dance on the wall, and the stairs seemed longer and darker than I remembered.

As I reached the top of the stairs, I saw a ghostly figure standing next to the door into the funeral home. The long white nightgown and long blonde hair glowed in the dim candlelight. For a minute my heart stopped. A ghost?

Then I knew. "Jen! What do you think you're doing?"

She turned around so fast she almost fell.

"Nothing. Nothing," she said guiltily.

Just then Gran burst out of my bedroom. "Where's Jennifer?" she demanded.

"Right here, trying to sneak into the funeral home," I snarled, so furious my blood felt hot in my veins. I hated Jennifer. She was stupid enough, reckless enough to go into the funeral home to scare us and get herself killed. Stupid. Stupid. Stupid. My face felt like I had a fever.

Before I could blurt out what I thought, Gran said coldly, "Jennifer, I would appreciate it if you would return to Leigh's room. We don't need any more of your tricks tonight."

Jen straightened her shoulders. For a minute I thought she was going to defy Gran, which could be her dumbest trick yet.

We stood silently watching one another in the shifting light of the candle. Jen's shoulder-length blonde hair shimmered, but her deep-set eyes were in shadow. She looked like she belonged in an Edgar Allan Poe poem in her long white nightgown, hair shining and secret eyes.

Then she smiled. "Hey, I'm sorry. It seemed like such a perfect chance, you know, the storm and the lightning and thunder and then the lights going out. I love it. It's just perfect."

Gran had to smile back at her. "Okay. I guess you're past helping, Jennifer Lawson, but I'm telling you now that all of you are staying right in Leigh's room where you belong for the rest of the night. Understood?"

Jen nodded, trying to look innocent. It didn't work.

"And as for you, young lady," Gran turned to me, "I want you in your room with your friends. I want all the monkeys in the cage."

"Mike told me to get the other kerosene lamp out of the guest room closet," I said weakly.

Maybe she could tell how much I dreaded going in the guest room alone because she said, "No. Let me have the candle and I'll go get the lamp. The flashlight in my bag doesn't work. The batteries must have worn out."

I grinned. I bet she had that flashlight in her overnight bag for the past ten years.

"You go in with the girls," Gran said. She turned to Jen. "And you, young lady, you better be in there when I get back with the lamp."

I felt almost faint with relief. Jen just grinned.

We went into the dark room, trying not to step on anyone. Almost no light came in through the windows. The rain beat down as if the house were sinking in the storm.

"Boy, West, this is one great party you planned for us. First we get scared to death. Then we get locked into your room with the warden. Now we can't even see each other. Thanks a lot."

I recognized the voice. "You're welcome, Lisa. I personally planned this storm. It's one of my best tricks." I thought about strangling her. If I could find her.

Just then Gran came in like Florence Nightingale, the lady with the lamp.

"Girls, I think it would be a good idea for all of you to bunk down now. Mike is back and there's a body in the funeral home, so no one can go in there."

Good one, Gran, I thought. The fact that the body was actually in the prep room wasn't really important.

Everyone grumbled a little, but some of us had to go to the Solo and Ensemble contest in the morning, so we really did need to try to get some sleep. I yawned big, and sure enough, it infected everyone. First Hilary and Molly yawned and pretty soon everyone was groaning, trying to keep from stretching their mouths to gasp for air.

I took my crumpled sleeping bag from where it had been tossed in the corner and put it down in front of the door.

"Great," Lisa said, sounding a lot like her mother, "now we have two guards."

"Shut up, Lisa," I said sweetly, "or I'll make you sleep here by the door where the living dead can grab you first."

Melissa and Amy snickered. Carrie moaned. "Please don't say that."

Lisa didn't answer. I flopped down on top of the bag and wondered how long the night was going to be.

Gran got ready to blow out the lamp. I noticed she had made her bed on the north window seat instead of my bed. Of course. That wacky old woman loves storms as much as Havoc hates them. She planned to sleep there so she could watch the lightning. I just hoped it wouldn't hit the maple and wipe her out.

Gran and Molly on the window seats, Lisa and Jen sharing the trundle. Hilary and Carrie in my bed. Holly and Stephanie in their sleeping bags at the foot of the bed, Melissa and Amy in front of the closet. Terrible. Ten, counting me. I wiggled down into my bag and reached into my pajama pocket to touch the skeleton key Matt had given me. Maybe it wouldn't work on my door, but I would try it as soon as I got the chance.

I heard Melissa whisper, "Leigh, I hope you aren't too mad at Amy and me."

"I'm not," I whispered back.

"Good," she and Amy said at the same time. I heard them wiggle around trying to get comfortable.

I waited as long as I could. It seemed like forever and week. Finally I thought, Okay. I'll try it.

I sat up and slipped the skeleton key into the old-fashioned lock. I held my breath, careful not to hit the side of the lock. I turned the key. There was a barely audible click. I waited. No one said anything. No one stirred.

I slipped the key out of the lock and put it back in my pocket. Now if we could just make it until morning, maybe I could get my friends out of here safely. Then I could worry about the stranger prowling through the funeral home, trapped in there by the alarms on the doors and windows and the locked doors to the family quarters.

Every time it thundered someone stirred. Slowly the flashes grew less frequent and the thunder farther away. Around three o'clock the storm stopped.

Around four the power came back on. I could see my guardian angel holding her lamb, and the light Gran must have turned on in the bathroom. No one moved. I wondered if I would ever sleep again.

Just then I heard something rub against the door. The knob turned. My heart took a big jump into my throat and banged away there so hard I thought I would choke.

I watched the knob, but it didn't turn a second time. Something rubbed against the door again. I wanted to scream, but I didn't dare. I just listened to my heart pound, my eyes too dry to cry. I wanted to run, and all I could do was lie still and pray no one kicked the door down.

Chapter Twenty Two

The endless night dragged on. When dawn began to shine through the windows every bone in my body hurt. My head ached. My fingernails had gouged holes in the palms of my hands, and I knew that when I looked in the mirror every hair on my head would be white.

I slipped the key out of my pocket, I slid it into the lock. The little click when I turned it wasn't nearly as loud as my heart.

Pushing my sleeping bag out of the way, I eased my door open and slipped out. Surely whatever I heard rubbing against the door in the night would be gone by now.

It wasn't. Matt sat sound asleep, leaning up against the wall with Mike's shotgun across his lap. Next to him was Havoc, big brown eyes watching me, tail thumping softly on the carpeted floor.

I crawled over and bent down to pet his beautiful head. Tears fell on his silver fur. "Oh, Havoc, are you okay?"

Matt answered me, sounding exhausted. "He's not perfect, but he's going to be all right."

My guardian brother looked awful, hair standing up like Dennis the Menace, big circles under his eyes, clothes all rumpled. The greatest looking guy in the world.

"Did Doc let you bring him home, or did you sneak him out?"

Matt shook his head. "She was waiting when I got there. She let me in, stayed a while, then left. I called her after the storm and told her I thought Havoc was better. She came over, checked on him, said I might as well bring him home." He smiled, "She said that way I wouldn't be calling at dawn to see how my dog was, and maybe she could get some sleep."

I grinned. Maybe life could get back to normal now. "Jed's home, too. He came flying in through the patio doors about the same time the lights went out."

Matt gave a half-hearted grin, and stood up carefully like he was afraid he was going to break. I knew how he felt. He tucked the shotgun under his arm and started for his room, Havoc leaning against his leg as he walked.

"Matt?"

"Yeah?"

"Where did you get the shotgun?"

He grinned. "In the back of the closet. I didn't have any shells, but I figured no one would know. So it might scare someone. You know."

I knew. It might scare someone trying to get into my room. "Thanks."

He nodded and stumbled to his bedroom.

Mumbling girls filed into my bathroom and Matt's. When the invasion began he just rolled over, put his arm around Havoc and went back to sleep. I hurried into his room ahead of the herd to move the shotgun, but Matt must have put it out of sight.

By the time I got downstairs Mom had set things out on the table, assorted cereals, toast, English muffins, donuts and a gallon of milk. I filled a bowl with Cheerios and milk and sat down.

Jen came bopping down, full of spit and vinegar as Gran would say. I really don't understand morning people. No day should start before 9:00 at the earliest. Personally, I can't think of anything to say before then anyway, so what's the use of getting up? Most of the others felt like me, so breakfast, except for good old Jen, was pretty quiet.

Her purple outfit hurt my morning eyes. A red sweatband around her head held her blonde hair back out of her eyes. She waved her toast at us. "I'll tell you one thing. When I die I want to be cremated and have my ashes scattered all over the football field. Then everyone who makes a touchdown will have to step right on top of me." She looked around at the girls, waiting for an answer. "None of this funeral home, casket, cemetery business for me." She took a bite of her toast.

A couple of the girls smiled half heartedly. It had been a long night. Then Carrie spoke, her voice soft as always, but suddenly firm. "You wouldn't feel that way if it was your mother."

No one said a word. Imagine Carrie challenging Jen! We all held our breath.

Jen looked surprised. She stared at Carrie. Carrie stared back. "If your mother died you'd want her body in a funeral home for a couple of days so you could see her face as long as you could. You'd want your friends to come and comfort you. You'd like to see the flowers that your mother would have loved. You wouldn't want to burn her up and throw her ashes out in a field."

She lowered her head so we couldn't see the tears.

"Or your brother," Hilary said softly. She took Carrie's hand.

Jen looked down at her toast. She swallowed hard, then said quietly. "You're right. I wouldn't. Sometimes I'm a jerk. I'm sorry."

One of those silences fell where no one knows what to say and everyone looks at the table or something. Any place but at the person talking.

Then Molly said, "Hey, how many of you are going to the solo and ensemble contest today?"

Stephanie, Holly and me.

"Leigh and I have to be there at 10:00," Molly said brightly. She looked at Mom. "Mrs. Pearson, will you drop me off at home so I can change?"

Mom smiled. She tried not to look relieved. "Of course. And I'll take the rest of you girls home as soon as you get your things gathered together."

Everybody got up and started back upstairs to get their stuff. Now was the time to tell Mom about what happened last night. I saw Gran watching me over the rim of her coffee cup.

"Where's Mike?" I asked. He should hear this too.

"He's checking the chapels. He got a call around 4:00 this morning. Estelle Brown killed herself yesterday. The police found her body in a motel in Richmond just after midnight. The coroner said it was suicide and released the body about an hour ago. We'll have visitation for her tomorrow."

"Is that Kippy Brown's mother?"

Mom nodded. "It's going to be hard on Kippy and her little brother."

Gran shook her head. "They'll have to go to live with their father and his new bride. It will be very difficult for them." She rubbed her forehead with her fingertips, "Estelle couldn't accept the divorce. I was afraid of something like this when she put the house up for sale." I heard the bitterness creep into her voice. "I tried to tell Jerry, but it was like talking to a brick wall."

She got up and walked out of the kitchen.

I swallowed hard. "Does Matt know?"

Mom nodded her head. "I hated to tell him. He liked Estelle. She must have taken fifty pictures of him and Kippy when they went to prom last year. She thought he was a good influence on Kippy."

I closed my eyes and wondered how regular people live. People who don't know when everyone dies. People who read the obituaries in the paper and turn the page. I thought about my brother sleeping upstairs, knowing that Kippy's mother was dead. I hated for Mom to find out that I hadn't told her the truth. I hated being scared and sad.

Mom looked at my face. "Is something bothering you, Leigh? Something more than Estelle?"

All the girls were upstairs. Gran was in the living room. We were alone. "Someone was in the funeral home last night."

Mom took a deep breath. "How do you know?"

"I saw a shadow when the girls were in the chapel, as if there was someone in the hallway. Later, when we were upstairs, someone turned the doorknob on the door into the funeral home."

Her face when white. "Oh, Leigh, why didn't you tell me then?"

"Because you would have sent the girls home and the story would have been all over town in five minutes. I couldn't be sure there really was anyone there, and besides, I knew they couldn't get out because of the alarms, and they couldn't get in here because we had all the doors locked."

It sounded pretty lame, even though I talked fast. Mom had one of those disappointed looks that always makes me feel like a chewed up shoe.

"You should have told me."

Just then the crew came roaring down the stairs. Mom got up from the table with one last long look at me. I felt worse and worse.

She led the girls to the garage, everyone talking at once, following her like ducklings. I sat at the table and wished I could go away somewhere, anywhere. I looked up when I felt Mom's hand on my hair. She stroked my head and smiled at me. "I love you , Leigh. I know you did what you thought was best. Go out and tell Mike right away. You and I will talk when I get back."

With that warning she turned and left.

Chapter Twenty Three

I stood at the door into the chapel. No one would be hiding there. Not in the daytime with Mike around. No one would be hiding there. Maybe if I kept repeating it to myself I would begin to believe it and my hands wouldn't feel like ice. Maybe I could breathe again.

Then I heard the growl of the vacuum. Marie cleaning the chapel. I turned the knob and pushed the door open.

She didn't turn around when I came in. I watched her wrinkled face, the color of moldy bread, like bodies before the makeup is put on. When did Marie get so old? She pushed the sweeper back and forth as if it took all the strength she had to move it. The faded blue kerchief she wore when she worked inched back off her head, the knot loose. Gray hair fell across her face. Her house dress hung on her.

I felt like crying. "Marie?"

She turned and saw me. She flipped the sweeper off with her foot. "Hello, Miss Leigh. How are you? Did you have fun at your party last night?"

I felt guilty. "Did we leave a mess?"

She smiled. "Not much. I got everything cleaned up pretty quick.'

"Are you okay, Marie?"

Her smiled faded. "Oh, sure. I'm fine, just fine. A little tired."

"How's Willy? Is he mowing today?"

"Mowing? No, he can't mow today. That bad storm last night. Too wet to mow. He's pulling weeds and setting some plants out to the side of the building."

"How's he feeling?" Besides grumpy and mean.

She frowned a little. "Not too good, Miss Leigh. It's his blood pressure medicine making him so tired all the time, and that other stuff he takes for depression. Makes him right irritable, on edge all the time. I think he ought to go back to the doctor and tell him he needs a different prescription or something, but he won't go. You know men."

I nodded as if I knew about men. So, Willy is tired and irritable. I wonder if he slid right over the edge and decided to poison our dog. I tried to sound casual, "Did your lights go out during the storm last night?" Or was Willy here sneaking around the funeral home?

She smiled. "Ours was out for a little while. But not like here. Mr. Pearson he said you didn't have lights for a couple of hours."

I nodded. "Did you have to get out the candles like we did?" And where was Willy when the lights went out?

"Oh, yes. Me and Willy lit our old kerosene lamp that was my daddy's when I was a little girl. We played us some cards till the television come back on."

I tried to smile. "I bet that was fun." So, old Willy hadn't been here during the storm, but he still might have been the one who let Jed out and poisoned Havoc. I couldn't figure out how to ask the right questions. Girl detective flunks first case.

"Is Mike in the office?"

Marie nodded. "Him and Dwight are in there getting things ready for tomorrow. It's too bad about that young mother. Mr. Mike told me about finding her down to that motel. Sad thing. Soon as I finish sweeping and dusting in here, it'll be ready for when they bring in the baskets of flowers and all."

I smiled a thanks and headed for the office to tell Mike the truth.

Dwight sat in the swivel chair behind the desk, twitching. Except for when he's with a family or working the door for a visitation Dwight twitches and jerks and pats the table or drums his fingers. I watched him stir the coffee in his half empty cup, round and round. His suit looked like he slept in his car for at least a week. "Where's Mike?"

Dwight frowned. "In the garage, washing the cars for tomorrow."

"Why is Mike doing that? Where's Willy?"

Dwight shrugged. "Came in and said he didn't feel good. I told him to work on the flowers."

"Right." I left him tapping his foot, stirring his coffee and flicking his cigarette lighter.

I found Mike in the garage. He turned from washing the coach, his sponge dripping soapy water on the cement floor. "Hi, Kid."

"I need to talk to you."

He looked at me, dropped the sponge into the bucket and said, "Shoot."

I told him about the shadow and the doorknob, talking fast.

He frowned. "So, if someone was in here, they couldn't leave without setting off the security system, and you kids had the doors locked into the quarters." He began to walk up and down, jingling the change in his blue jeans pocket. He looked different in jeans. When he worked on the door, or met families, he always wore a dark suit and looked real professional. I liked the jeans look best.

I had to ask. "Do you believe me?

"Believe you? Of course. Something is going on around here, and whatever it is, it's serious. Havoc is proof of that. Maggie saw strangers at the service yesterday. Maybe they didn't leave with the others. One or all of them could have stayed around, hiding. Whoever was in here could have sneaked out as soon as we turned the alarms off this morning."

"What are we going to do?"

He began pacing and jingling again. "We need to hook up the VCR with the video monitor at the front door. That way we can check the tape after Estelle Brown's visitation and see who comes." He nodded to himself.

"Would you mind dressing up and working the door at the Brown visitation tomorrow? You can hang up coats. That way you can keep an eye out for strangers. Matt can help too. He can be sure everyone signs the book. You go into the service and keep your eyes peeled. Matt can stay in the vestibule and make sure no one tries to sneak out. Dwight and I will be seating people and checking things out."

I nodded. It was kind of frightening to be asked to help, but exciting too. "I have to go get ready for the solo and ensemble contest at the university, but I'll be back this afternoon."

Mike nodded, and tried to sound normal and interested when he asked, "So, what are you entered in today?"

"I'm playing piano for Molly when she does her flute solo, and then I've got a sax duet with Stephanie at 11:00. They announce the winners around 1:00, so I ought to be back before 2:00. Matt is going to pick me up."

He was already thinking of other things. "Good luck."

Yeah. It would be a nice change.

I changed my clothes, got my sax and my music and went out to the van that Mom parked by the side of the garage when she came back from delivering the girls. Willy was kneeling in the flower bed, pulling weeds. He didn't look up. I thought of Marie, so tired and thin, just the way Carrie's mom looked before she died.

"Hello, Willy."

He didn't look up. I felt my face go red. I wanted to yell at him. Did you poison our dog? I cleared my throat and yelled, "Hello, Willy!"

Mom looked surprised. Willy raised his head and glared at me. "Hello," he muttered.

I climbed into the van, holding my music carefully, and wished Mom would turn the wheel and run over the old goat.

On the way to the university Mom asked, "Why did you yell at Willy?"

"Because he's rude and mean, and Marie looks terrible. Do you think he poisoned Havoc?"

Mom shook her head. "I don't want to think that. Willy's been with Mike a long time. But, who knows." She paused, then asked, "Did you talk to Mike?"

I told her what Mike said. "He wants me and Matt to stand at the door during Kippy's mother's visitation."

"I don't know, Leigh. I hate for you kids to get mixed up in all this. I'm not sure it's safe."

I frowned, feeling that lump in my throat again. "We're already mixed up in it, Mom. Havoc was poisoned, Jed was let out, Matt's tire was slashed."

"I know." I could tell she wasn't happy. "I wish I had some answers."

Yeah, me too.

At the contest chaos reigned, as usual. Kids ran up and down the halls, searching for their rooms, hauling instruments, looking frantic. Molly played her flute almost perfectly, and I played piano for her as well as I ever had. A Superior rating for sure.

She must have felt the same way because she kept complaining the way people do when they expect to win. "I think I played the seventh measure a little too fast, don't you?"

I grinned. "You were great. You'll get a First, period."

She smiled back. She knew I was right.

My duet with Stephanie slid into the dust, out at second base. Maybe we were just too tired after the slumber party. We walked down the hall bumping into other musicians, all of them hurrying to their rounds, not looking where they were going.

"What was that note I hit?" Stephanie asked.

"I think it was in the crack between B and C."

She groaned. "I tell you, West, these funeral home slumber parties will kill you."

"Funny," I said. "Very funny."

The ratings didn't surprise us. Molly got a Superior. Stephanie and I got ribbons for participation. Thanks a lot.

I found Molly talking on the pay phone. "Ready to go home, Champ?"

She looked at me, then back at the phone. "Trevor is going to pick me up in a few minutes," she whispered.

I felt my face get stiff. "Oh." I waited, I don't know for what. Molly watched me. "Well, okay," I said, surprised to sound almost normal. "I better go. Matt's probably waiting for me."

I turned to leave. "Don't be mad at me, Leigh. I'm just letting Trevor take me home. It's no big deal."

I didn't turn around. "Hey, no problem. I'll see you."

"Leigh," Molly called, "Are you still going to take the job at the Sweet Shoppe with me?"

I hadn't thought about it. There was too much going on to worry about the Sweet Shoppe. I shrugged.

Matt had the engine running when I came out. I put my sax and music in the back seat and climbed into the Nova. I fastened my seat belt and locked the door. He looked at me and asked, "You okay?"

"Sure."

"Where's Molly?"

"She's riding home with Trevor Lewis." I thought I sounded natural.

"Oops," Matt said softly as he put the car into gear. After a couple of blocks he asked, "Did you talk to Mike?"

I nodded.

"Me, too."

"What do you think about us working the door?" I asked.

"I don't know. I'm willing. But I don't know if I could stop someone who tried to leave the service."

I shook my head. "I don't think Mike expects you to wrestle with anyone. He just wants you to say, 'Hey, where do you think you're going?' or something."

"I'll practice that. Yeah. Hey, where do you think you're going or something?"

"Clever. So I'm riding with a stand up comedian."

"Wrong again, butthead. I'm sitting down."

He stopped talking and drove back to the funeral home. Before I got out I said, "I'm sorry about Kippy's mom."

"Yeah. Me, too. I just wish I could do something."

I knew what he meant. So much craziness and there wasn't anything we could do. It was a rotten feeling.

Chapter Twenty Four

Saturday was the longest day in history. Mike and Matt checked the funeral home for signs someone had been hiding inside during the night. I tagged along.

Mike opened the door to the attic. I shuddered when he touched the doorknob. I could still feel it turn in my hand.

With all the lights flipped on the attic didn't look quite so scary, except for the dress form in the corner and the wooden heads with plastic wrapped hats on top of an old dresser. I was looking at the heads when I heard Matt whistle. "Hey, look at this."

I tiptoed over and saw ashes and two ground out cigarettes scattered over the floor next to the old horse-hair couch. "Wow," I whispered. "He could have burned the place down."

Mike nodded, looking grim. "I'm going to call Harold."

I moaned a little, but Matt gave me a fierce look so I didn't say anything about Barney Fife.

Harold came right away, all dressed up in his beige sheriff's uniform, wearing his badge and a big gun over his fat belly. It made me nervous to think of him with that gun. Maybe he only had one bullet.

When they back down from the attic, Mom offered Harold a cup of coffee. He nodded, very serious for Harold. He cleared his throat, "You folks are in the city limits. I think you ought to call the police and notify them, too."

Mike rubbed his forehead. He was doing that a lot lately. "I don't know, Harold. You know how gossip spreads in a town this size. If we get the police in here we might as well take out an ad in the paper."

Harold frowned, big wrinkles creasing the fat on his face. "That's true. But this is durned unusual, my friend. Who do you reckon was hiding in your attic? And why?"

Mike shook his head. "If we know why, we'd know who."

Harold set his coffee cup down. "I'll call home and tell Alice I'm staying the evening here. I'll leave the county car parked in plain sight under the overhang. You got any calling hours here today? Any legit reason for a stranger to get in?"

"Nothing until tomorrow. We can set the alarms later and hope for the best," Mike said.

Things changed in the afternoon. That happens a lot in a funeral home. People don't plan the day of their deaths.

Mike came into the quarters where Mom was fixing dinner, making special things for Harold, who was eating with us. I was glad she was making plenty.

"I'm going to have to go to Indianapolis again. Harry Friedman died in Ohio and they're shipping him back tonight. We have to have the funeral tomorrow."

"Tomorrow?" Mom asked. "Tomorrow's Sunday. We never have funerals on Sunday."

"I know. But Harry is Jewish and he has to be buried within 24 hours of his death. I've called Roselawn and they'll open and close the grave tomorrow for a double rate."

Mom just shook her head.

"Is that the man who owns Friedman Jewelry Store down town?" I asked.

"Yes. He was a fine man. Well thought of around here. His brother Frank is making all the arrangements. I've ordered the special wooden casket."

"Wooden?"

"No metal at all, no screws or bolts. It's all held together with pegs. It'll be here in the morning. There won't be any flowers, either."

"Why?"

"Well, Leigh, different people have different customs. That's just the way it is. The body won't be embalmed either, so the casket will be closed."

The rest of the day seemed almost normal. We locked the funeral home, checked all the doors and windows, set the alarms and went into the quarters. Gran called and talked to Mom for a long time.

When Mom finished fixing supper, she set out the good china because Harold was eating with us. Matt looked at the table, amazed. "Wow. The good china. I thought it was only for the president."

Mom gave him a cool look. "I don't think we need to use it every day. It's for special occasions."

"Like Harold?" I asked.

"Like Harold," she said firmly.

Matt touched one of the gold-rimmed dinner plates. "That's too bad. I kind of thought that every day we ate together was special. Like in Our Town."

Mom gave him a funny look. "I swear, Matthew, you've been different ever since you were in that play."

He shrugged. "Maybe it just made me think."

It made me think, too.

I got so fascinated watching Harold eat that I almost forgot to feed myself. He could put away more food than Matt, who was still growing. Of course, Harold was still growing, too, just out instead of up.

"Great cake, Maggie," Harold said as he ate his third piece. I caught Matt's eye and looked away fast, before we both started laughing.

Matt and I did the dishes. I washed. He dried. No argument. "Maybe it wouldn't be such a good thing to eat off these every day," he said. "You can't put them in the dishwasher."

I was putting the good silverware in the chest while Matt finished drying the last of the pans when we heard Havoc growl. He was standing at the patio doors looking out. Harold pulled out his gun and slid the door open. Havoc rushed past him barking. When Harold got outside, Havoc had his paws on the gate, barking his fiercest sound.

Before we got the gate open we heard the sound of a car engine start and a car drive away. Havoc raced off after the sound, but Matt called him back.

When we got back in the house Havoc gave Matt a dirty look. Matt squatted down and hugged him. "You're a good dog. You would have chased that car to China, wouldn't you?"

I think Havoc nodded.

"Well," Harold said, "that sure explains why someone wanted to poison your dog."

Around 8:30 Mike and Harold got ready to leave for Indianapolis to get Harry Friedman's body. Harold left the cruiser parked under the overhang, visible from the street. "Could make an intruder think twice," he said.

Mom checked her watch. "It's pretty early for you to leave. The plane won't be in until 11:00. What's the hurry?"

Mike looked sheepish, like he had a secret. Mom kept staring at him. Finally he said, "Last night when we got to the airport to pick up Larry Novak there were a couple of men there with a van. They said they were supposed to pick up a body, but when the cargo was unloaded, Novak's body was the only one on the plane."

Mom's eyes were big. "What happened?"

"At first I thought they were going to try to take it, but I had all the papers and when I threatened to call the state police, they left."

Mike shook his head. "I don't know, but two days is too many. I'm going to talk to Gertrude Hamilton tomorrow. All this started with Novak, and I want to know why."

While we waited for Mike and Harold to get back, Mom and Matt and I pretended we were watching television, but I don't remember a single thing we saw that night. Around midnight we heard them bringing the casket into the garage.

When they came into the house Harold cleared his throat. "No problems tonight. If you think it's okay, I'd kind of like to bunk down here tonight. No sense stomping in so late and bothering Alice. What about it, Maggie?"

I saw Mom and Mike exchange glances. "Sure," she said. "We'd be glad to have you. You can sleep in the guest room upstairs."

"Oh, that's too much trouble. I'll just pile down here on the couch. Maybe go up with you and make sure all the doors are locked." He gave an actor's grin that made me even more nervous.

The doors were all secure. The red light of the security alarm flashed and the beeping began as we closed the last door.

Matt went to his room. Mom and Mike and Harold told me goodnight as I started up the stairs. Everything was all right, locked up tight and safe. Sure it was.

I stood at the edge of my window and looked out at the woods. I heard the wild dogs barking faintly in the distance. I could see Roselawn, mysterious in the moonlight. One of the monuments moved. I caught my breath and watched. No. Not the angel. Someone stepped from behind the big stone. Someone dim and hard to see, even in the moonlight. The figure faced the funeral home, head raised as if he were looking at me, as if he could see me clearly in my dark room watching him.

I started to go downstairs to tell Harold but the figure slipped back behind the monument and disappeared.

Chapter Twenty Five

The Friedman funeral ended the family tradition of grilling out while we listened to the big race. The Indy 500 started at 11:00 on Sunday. By then everything had been set up Kippy's mother's visitation in the evening, and in the small chapel things were ready for Mr. Friedman. Chairs in place, podium at the side of the all-wood casket just in from New York. The register book and memorial folders were on the lighted podium at the entrance to the chapel. Three baskets of flowers looked as if some of the customers from the jewelry store didn't know the rules for a Jewish funeral.

A 14 X 20 framed portrait of Mr. Friedman stood on an easel next to the closed casket. Looking at his kind face made the body in the casket seem real to me for the first time. I blinked my eyes to keep the tears back and wondered how Mike could do this every day.

There was no regular visitation. The funeral was scheduled at 2:00. About 1:30 the rabbi from Indianapolis came in with an elderly man in a wheelchair. Mike introduced Frank Friedman, Harry Friedman's older brother.

Frank Friedman looked like parchment, and his mottled hands kept gripping the arm rests on his wheelchair. He wore a yarmulke, a small skull cap. I had never seen one before. I tried not to stare.

"Hello, Mr. Friedman," I said when Mike introduced us. He looked up at me and tried to smile, but didn't speak. A tear rolled down his left cheek unnoticed. The rabbi rolled him into the chapel where he sat looking at the portrait of his brother.

From then on people kept streaming in. Then I saw him, Clarence Modrine, all cleaned up, shaved, hair combed, in an ancient suit that smelled of moth balls. I swallowed hard. "Mr. Modrine," I said.

He looked at me blindly as if he had never seen me before or yelled at me, as if he couldn't quite remember where he was.

"Frank is my friend," he said, as if I had asked him why he was there. "We went to school together. This will be very hard for him."

I nodded.

"He loved Harry. Raised him, you know, after their parents died. Frank was always so proud of Harry. This will be very hard for him."

I nodded again, feeling my throat tighten.

He looked at me, seeing me for the first time. "Are you Pearson's daughter?"

"No, sir. I'm his step-daughter Leigh."

He seemed to think that over. "Well, he's a good man, Michael Pearson. Sometimes I don't like the traffic over here. I tell him."

I nodded one more time, not sure what to say, but wishing I could think of something to make him feel better.

"But it's an important service he does, young lady. We have to have someone to help us when people die. He's a good man. This is going to be very hard for Frank."

"Mr. Friedman is already here, if you'd like to go in," Mike said gently from behind me.

Mr. Modrine looked toward the chapel. "Yes, This is going to be very hard for Frank." He moved slowly away from us, then turned around. A smile twitch of his lips might have been a smile. "You are a pretty young woman, and polite. I like that." He looked hard at Mike. "You should be very proud of her."

"I am, sir. I am."

I hate this business, I thought. How can I ever make fun of that poor old man again?

Just before the service more people showed up. We directed, smiled a little, but not too much, had everyone write in the register book. I looked at everyone who came in, wondering which one might be a dog poisoner, tire slasher.

Just before 2:00 a man came in who reeked STRANGER. Fairly tall, maybe 5'11", slender like a runner, dark eyes, black hair cut by an expert, wearing a fancy suit that cost more than the Nova.

"Are you here for the Friedman service?" Matt asked. The man nodded but didn't speak to us.

"Would you please sign the register?" Matt said it pleasantly, just the way he was supposed to. The two of them made eye contact and I saw Matt pull in his breath as the guy in the expensive suit hesitated. Then the man picked up the pen and signed the book. I wanted to run over and check it out, but I stood still and waited.

He walked past me into the chapel. He smelled wonderful, kind of smoky and leathery and expensive. This man is not from Modrine, Indiana, I thought, not in a hundred light years. I was careful not to exchange glances with my brother who was acting as cool as if every day of his life he asked strangers who looked like gangsters to sign the register book.

As soon as the guy went into the chapel and Matt and I were alone, I checked the book. "Ross Geller." I almost laughed.

Matt read it over my shoulder. "He doesn't look like he's on Friends."

I shrugged. "At least he didn't sign it Mel Gibson or Michael Jackson."

I slipped into the back of the chapel and sat down…right next to Geller himself. My, but he did smell good, and he had this sexy dimple in his chin. He gave me an quick look and then turned back to watch the rabbi who had begun to sing in Hebrew.

The service lasted approximately twenty minutes. People who knew Harry Friedman stood and spoke briefly. From my place in the back I couldn't understand what Frank Friedman said, but somehow the sadness in his soft words brought tears to my eyes. Then the rabbi recited the 23rd psalm. He finished with a memorial prayer and the Kaddish, the prayer for the dead. I had never been to a Jewish funeral before, but with all the differences, it was so much the same, solemn, and full of grief, and final. It got to me.

As I wiped my nose with a tissue, out of the corner of my left eye I saw Geller rising. He stepped past me and out the door. Matt, I thought, stop him!

Usually Mike and Dwight go out to the coach while the pallbearers remove the casket, but this time they ushered us out of the chapel. I slipped out the door and saw Geller the Mobster standing toe to toe with my brother, who was pale, but composed.

Others filed out before I could get over to hear what was going on. Mr. Modrine came up to me, "No one sits Shiva anymore."

I turned to look at him and smiled. He must have seen the question in my eyes.

"In the old days, when we had a temple here and a rabbi and a congregation for my Jewish friends, a week was set aside to mourn. In the house they covered the mirrors with black cloths." He sighed. "You don't look on the living in the face of death. So friends came to visit and eat and talk. It was good for the heart. It helped with the pain."

He studied my face. "Everything changes. The old ways die. But are the new ones better?" He shook his head. "I will go to visit Frank this week. I'll take some food. We'll talk. It will be good for him."

I didn't answer. He didn't need an answer.

Mike came up to where Matt and the stranger were standing. "Sir, are you planning to go to the burial?"

The man glared at him. "No, I'm not." He turned and walked out.

I waited until the last visitor left before I asked Matt, "What did you say to him? Man you guys were talking a long time!"

"I said 'Where do you think you're going or something?" Matt frowned. "That guy was determined to go on into the funeral home. I don't know what he wanted, but there was a minute there when I really thought he was going to belt me. Talk about mean."

I looked at skinny Matt. "Well, big brother, you were standing right up to him."

Matt grinned. "Yeah, I was."

Chapter Twenty Six

After the Friedman funeral and before the evening visitation for Estelle Brown, Matt, Kevin, Dwight, Mike, Mom and I took turns sitting in the vestibule. Mike locked up, but we couldn't lock the front door in case someone wanted to come in early. That happens a lot.

Kippy's mom lay in the big chapel. Maybe she wasn't a power lady like Gertrude Hamilton, but Kippy's mom worked in her church, in the PTA, Altrusa and the League of Women Voters, so lots of people knew her.

Matt stayed pretty quiet until I asked him, "What are you thinking?"

He gave me a look. "I'm thinking that a lot of the gossips will be wondering why Mrs. Brown OD-ed in a motel room." His voice took on a mocking tone, "Do you suppose she never got over the divorce? Do you suppose it was the kids? Maybe she had a terminal illness. Maybe, maybe, maybe. They make me sick."

"Mike said she cleaned her house from top to bottom and gave away a bunch of stuff the last couple of weeks."

"Kippy told me she registered under her own name at the motel. Maybe she wanted someone to stop her. But why did she wait until Kippy left to sneak off? I mean, who knows what was going on," Matt said.

"Maybe she had some terrible disease and wanted to spare her kids."

Matt glared at me. "See, you're doing it right now. Maybe she just got fed up with the world."

I shut up.

Kippy came early and Matt walked into the chapel with her. She hung on his arm like her legs were weak, and I thought about Carrie talking to us about how you feel when your mother dies. Kippy would feel that way now, and forever. I was glad Dwight had done such a good job, so the casket could be open and Kippy could see her mother's face these last few hours.

Mom came in to relieve me. "Do you think I could have some of the pineapple upside down cake that's left over from the feast you served Harold last night?"

Mom looked puzzled. "Of course, you can have some of the cake. Why did you even think you had to ask?"

I felt the color rush up to my cheeks. "Well, I wanted to take a couple of pieces over to Mr. Modrine."

Mom tried not to smile. "You mean Old Man Modrine?"

I wouldn't meet her eyes. "He seems lonely," I muttered.

"He probably is, and the cake is a wonderful idea. Go wrap up what's left and take it over to him."

In the kitchen I found a big plastic-coated plate that looked like china. I slid the cake off the crystal server onto the plate and covered it with aluminum foil. It made a shiny, cheerful package. I hummed a little of You are my Sunshine and Havoc joined in with a whine. I laughed. "Hey, fella, that's not real singing."

I swear he understood every word. He cocked his head and looked at me, then threw back his head and began to howl with me. We did part of the chorus before Mom came flying in from the funeral home.

"Leigh Allison West! What on earth are you doing?"

"Singing with Havoc," I said.

"That's one name for it." She opened the patio doors and ordered Havoc outside. "Take that cake across the street before you get Jed started too."

On cue Jed cried, "Leeeeeeeee. Leeeeeee." Wolf whistle. "Oh, baby, baby, baby, baby."

Mom took my shoulders and pointed me toward the adjoining doors. "Go through the little chapel. Kippy is already here."

I felt awful. "Oh, Mom, I forgot. I'm sorry. Should I go apologize? I just forgot. I saw her come in."

Mom patted my arm. "It's okay. I doubt she even heard. I'll cover Jed so he'll stay quiet, and you deliver your cake."

I stopped at the double doors into the chapel. "Mom, how did Mr. Modrine turn from a wacky old maniac to a lonely old man in one afternoon?"

She smiled at me. "He didn't change, Leigh. You did."

Chapter Twenty Seven

Across the street Mr. Modrine's yard looked like the Before picture in a gardening magazine. I wondered what it would take to make it look like After. A small army maybe, with clippers, trimmers, hoes, rakes and mowers. Maybe I could talk Matt into doing a little free work for Mr. Modrine. Free. For nothing. Probably not, but it was worth asking.

I walked up to the front door, pushing past the evergreens that touched across the walk, ducking under a low branch on one of those warped trees that grew from weeds. I didn't see a doorbell so I raised the blackened brass door knocker and dropped it against the heavy door. Nothing. I banged it down again. Nothing. I stood there holding my aluminum foil package feeling like an idiot. Maybe he was in there looking out. Maybe he didn't want company. Maybe he was as nuts as I always thought.

Too many maybes. So, maybe he was around back and couldn't hear the knocker. Everybody knew the house was going to become a county museum when Mr. Modrine died. Maybe sound didn't carry really well in a house big enough to be a museum. Maybe I should go around to the back door.

Nuts to wondering. I pushed my way through the shrubs that kept catching on my shirt, feeling like the prince trying to find Sleeping Beauty. The thought of Mr. Modrine as a sleeping beauty cracked me up. Molly will love it, I thought. Then I remembered that she was probably out with Trevor Lewis that very minute and the joke didn't seem so funny. I headed around the house.

At the back the bushes and shrubs grew higher and even closer together than around the front. I wove my way through the path on a defeated looking broken sidewalk.

The storm door stood slightly ajar. The screen hadn't been put in. I looked through the streaked glass of the storm and realized this wasn't the door to the house; it led to a big porch. I grabbed the door handle to keep the door steady and knocked as hard as I could, but the sound didn't seem to carry. I let go of the handle and the door swung open again.

I tried to decide what to do. I didn't want to go back home with the cake and I really, really didn't want to go in on that porch and knock at the back door of the house. Miss Courage.

I went in. The porch had more stuff than a flea market. I saw an old pie safe that still had the metal plates on the front, a couple of carved marble-topped tables piled high with plates and bowls stacked up like the Leaning Tower of Pisa, tons of magazines, boxes stacked on top of boxes, buckets, double wash tubs and at least a dozen brown crocks. Garage sale paradise.

I knocked on the back door. It wasn't locked either, and swung open when I knocked, like one of those horror movies where the girl finds each door opening in front of her—an invitation to murder.

My neck felt tight and all the little hairs stood on end. What should I do now? I always thought those girls who keep on going down basements with a candle were a week past stupid. Now I was one of them. I took another step. Maybe if I yell.

"Mr. Modrine!" No answer.

Then I heard a pounding sound. Thud. Thud. Thud.

"Mr. Modrine!" I called louder.

The thudding came faster.

"Mr. Modrine, is that you?" Faintly I heard a moaning sound. Maybe he'd fallen and couldn't get up and didn't have one of those life-saving things they advertise on television. I swallowed hard. Going into that house to look for him ranked lower than going down the basement in the funeral home.

I stepped farther into the kitchen, holding onto the cake for dear life. "Mr. Modrine?"

The thudding continued, and the moaning. The sound came from behind a door on my left. The swinging door looked like the one to the pantry at Great-Grandmother Ethel's old house. I stepped toward the door with my heart pounding even louder than the thumping coming from the other side. I didn't want to be doing this.

I pushed the swinging door to look in the pantry. Something kept the door from swinging in. I pulled it toward me until it clicked open. Mr. Modrine was lying on the floor, and he really couldn't get up. No one could have, not with silver tape on his ankles and wrists and across his mouth.

I put the cake down on the floor and knelt down next to him to take the tape off his mouth. That was when I saw the blood on his head, clotting his thin white hair.

Just then the swinging door slammed into me, knocking me flat next to Mr. Modrine. We lay side by side on the floor of the pantry, surrounded by shelves of canned goods and dishes. I saw his eyes. He looked terrified.

"Leigh. Hey, Leigh. Are you in there?" It was Matt's voice, from outside.

"Matt," I screamed, scrambling up, "go call the police and an ambulance. Hurry!!"

I heard the screen door slam and knew Matt was running top speed to call the police. Thank you, God, for a brother who can run fast and doesn't need to talk things over before he moves.

I reached for the tape one more time. Then I heard the screen door slam again. "Matt?" No answer.

"Matt is that you?"

No answer. Then I knew. It was whoever had done this to Mr. Modrine, getting away. It was the person who slammed me with the swinging door, the person who would have taped me up too, or killed me if Matt hadn't come.

I felt like my fingers were mittens as I tried to pull the silver tape off Mr. Modrine's mouth. He flinched and I saw tears in his eyes. I wanted to cry. "I'm sorry."

"No. No. It's okay, young lady," he said weakly. "Is he gone? I heard the door slam."

"I think so. My brother's gone for help. Who did this to you?" I squatted next to him and pulled as gently as I could on the tape that held his writs.

"I don't know who it was. Someone hit me from the back. Someone was waiting for me when I got back from Harry's funeral."

I shuddered. I had the tape off his wrists and tried to rub them as easily as I could. He moved his fingers experimentally and sighed. I began to work on the tape around his ankles, but it was wrapped tight.

"I think it was the same person who was hiding in the house Friday night. The police didn't find anyone, but I know what I heard," his voice sounded stronger, but he lay very still on the floor.

He stopped talking and closed his eyes again while I kept at the tape. Suddenly he opened his eyes and gave me a fierce look. "Just what are you doing here?"

I looked at his angry face. Oh, no, I thought, he's turning into Mr. Hyde right in front of me.

"I came to bring you some pineapple upside down cake," I said, feeling betrayed by his anger.

He raised his head a little and looked at the aluminum foil package on the floor next to his feet. As fast as it came, his anger faded. "How nice," he murmured. "What a nice thing to do."

He put his head back down. He spoke again with his eyes still closed. His voice sounded weak. "That was a very nice thing to do. I can't remember when anyone has brought me a pineapple upside down cake. Maybe never."

I pulled some more of the tape off his ankles, my hands trembling so much I could hardly hold on to the sticky stuff.

"Leigh!" It was Mom.

"In here. In the pantry."

She and Mike pushed the door against my back, then pulled it toward them so they could see us. Mom knelt down by me. "Mr. Modrine, are you all right?"

He didn't open his eyes. "No. As you can clearly see, I'm severely injured, dizzy as a dodo bird, and not at all prepared to entertain guests at the moment."

I wanted to cry and grin at the same time.

"However, if I were so inclined," he whispered, lying still as death, "I could offer guests a piece of pineapple upside cake, thanks to this brave young lady." He didn't open his eyes, but I saw him smile.

Mom smiled too, but her eyes were shining with tears.

The sirens wailed closer and closer. I had the tape off and rolled up into a big silver ball.

Mike and the paramedics waved me and Mom out of the pantry. After a few minutes, apparently satisfied it was safe to move him, they lifted him carefully onto a stretcher and began to wheel him out of the pantry. He opened his faded black eyes and looked at me. "Take care of my cake, young lady. I'll eat it when I get home." He closed his eyes again and they carried him out of the house.

"Yes, sir," I said softly, hoping he didn't see the tears.

Mike was outside talking to Harold when Mom and I followed the paramedics out to the ambulance.

Harold's face was more serious than I had ever seen it. "We'll leave someone here to guard the house. You realize that if Leigh hadn't come over here he probably would have died in the pantry. With his reputation no one would have come looking for him for weeks."

It was too much. Before I could stop, I burst into tears, sobbing so hard that my chest hurt. Mom pulled me into her arms and held me. She kept patting my back and saying, "Leigh. Oh, Leigh baby."

But even as I cried some part of me noticed that she didn't say, "It'll be all right." I knew why. She didn't think it would be, and neither did I.

Chapter Twenty Eight

We walked back to the funeral home. I wouldn't let Mom carry the cake, but I did let her keep her arm around my shoulders. Usually I hate that, but right then I didn't mind so much.

Dwight waited for us inside the front door, pacing up and down, flicking his lighter and looking worried. He took my shoulders and looked me straight in the face. "Are you okay, kid?"

"Sure," I said, trying to sound adult and brave. Then I sniffed and ruined the whole thing. I knew I was a mess, eyes red and nose running, dirt ground into my good peach dress from rolling around on the pantry floor. I probably wiped up dust that had been there since the Civil War.

Dwight hugged me and Mom patted my back one last time. "Why don't you go and clean up a little?" She turned and looked at Mike. Her voice was cold. "I don't think she needs to be watching for strangers this evening, do you?"

Mike looked straight at Mom, but his face flushed. She didn't talk to him in that tone of voice very often. I knew it was because she was scared about what happened to me at Mr. Modrine's. I was scared, too, but I hated to see Mike embarrassed.

"No," he said quietly, "she's been through too much." He came up to me and lifted my chin so I was looking him right in the eye. "Leigh, I would never have let you take that cake over there if I thought there was any danger."

I nodded. I knew that. Mom knew it, too. She flushed a little, then smiled at him. "I know you wouldn't, Mike. I'm just scared for her."

He put his arm around her and she leaned against him the same way I leaned against her. "It'll be all right, Maggie," he said. But he didn't sound like he believed it any more than I did.

Alone in my room I looked out at Roselawn. Usually I thought the cemetery was beautiful, but today the tall stones in the old part looked like the crooked teeth of a beast coming up out of the ground. In the fading light the three white mausoleums glowed in the setting sun, the angels in front beckoning. I hated it.

A cry from the woods made my hair stand on end. A howl and a yip and a cry all at once. Coyotes. Two sheep had been killed at the Peterson farm. Nothing safe in the beautiful woods. Predators roamed free and the weak were their prey. Listening to the howling I felt like a fawn with no place to hide.

The phone rang. Maybe it was Molly. I hadn't talked to her since the solo and ensemble contest. I wanted to tell her about Mr. Modrine. So what if she liked Trevor Lewis. "Hello." No one answered. "Hello," I said again.

Someone breathed heavily in my ear. I slammed the phone back in its cradle and burst into tears again. I threw myself across the bed, sobbing.

I must have gone right to sleep, because I can't remember anything except the dream. I was moving through the funeral home as fast as I could. Someone was after me. When I turned around to look behind me, I saw Mr. Modrine, except he looked like Willy. Then he ran past me and I was by the front doors where Mike showed us the secret alarm. I knew that if I could just pull that red lever, everything would be okay. In the distance someone called my name. "Leeeeeee. Leeeeeee." I knew it wasn't Matt or Jed. The caller was someone evil who wanted to hurt me.

Even in the dark I could make out the words Ellis and Pearson. I thought that was funny. It should say Ellis Brothers. I pulled the wooden plaque to one side and grabbed the rusty red lever. My heart pounded fiercely as a bass drum.

I heard a small creak, footsteps of someone creeping up on me, or someone opening the door to the Prep room. "The living are more dangerous than the dead," someone said close to my ear. I screamed and woke up, shaking.

My room was dark, barely lit by the security light that cut through the windows like a thin-bladed knife. I shivered, chilled to the bone, and wondered what time it was.

Half-past eight by the digital clock next to my angel. Half-past eight. The visitation for Estelle Brown started at seven. I should have been down there to look for strangers, but I didn't move. I was glad I wasn't downstairs. I didn't want to see any strangers. I didn't want to see Kippy Brown or her dad. Jerry Brown was probably the reason Kippy's mother had taken the pills. Maybe not. The world was too full of maybes.

I got up and went to the bathroom to wash up. I tossed my ruined dress down on the floor. Matt says, "Give Mom a zebra and she'll turn it into a palomino." But when I looked at the filth on the peach skirt, I didn't think anything could save it. I pushed it away with my foot.

My navy blue sweats suited my mood. I washed my face and brushed my teeth and heard my stomach growl. I had slept through supper. I leaned against the sink and pressed my forehead against the mirror. Get it together, girl.

Downstairs the family quarters were empty. Watching for strangers, I guessed. The TV mumbled something about the race and I realized we hadn't even thought about it all day. The Indy 500—over and done with for another year and for the first time I could remember we didn't listen to it on the radio. Nothing was right.

I found the peanut butter and sweet pickles and tried not to think about anything as I spread the peanut butter on a slice of whole wheat bread. Mom startled me when she came in from the chapel with a tall, tanned woman I had never seen before. Now we're entertaining the strangers.

"Jillian," Mom said, "this is my daughter Leigh. Leigh, Jillian Montgomery."

Jillian. She had to be Larry Novak's mother. The one who lost custody to his father. Gertrude Hamiliton's daughter who used to date my Uncle Joe, who didn't really love her all that much.

I nodded. "Hello."

She smiled at me with teeth that glittered against her tan. I wondered if she ever read the warnings about too much sun. She was going to be pure leather in about five years if she didn't get skin cancer first. Maybe she didn't read.

"Would you like a cup of tea?" Mom asked.

"That would be lovely.'

I kept fixing my sandwich, waiting for Mom to order me out of the room so they could talk. Instead she asked me to sit down and join them. Ms. Montgomery looked unhappy. I liked that.

"Leigh has been involved in all the unpleasant things going on around her, Jillian. It's important for her to hear what you have to say. I don't think it's fair to exclude her now."

Jillian Montgomery nodded but didn't speak until the tea was ready and Mom pulled out a chair and sat down. "I came because I'm concerned about my son's funeral tomorrow. Have any of his family from Chicago contacted you?"

Mom shook her head. "Not that I know of."

Jillian stirred her tea, looking for an answer in the steaming cup. Her nails were the same dusty rose as her lipstick. A small gold band gleamed on the index finger of her right hand, an enormous diamond on the ring finger of her left. A gold watch spun loosely around on her left wrist, two gold bracelets on her right arm matched her earrings and necklace. Her beige sheath dress and her perfume reeked expensive. I thought about Gran's words, "Some women have understated elegance. It comes with Old Money." Looking at Jillian Montgomery sitting in our kitchen drinking tea, I felt poor, stupid and clumsy.

She clenched her hands together and began to speak. "Maggie, do you remember when I left to go to New York, stars in my eyes, ready for the big time?"

Mom smiled and nodded. "We all thought you'd make it."

"So did I." She sighed. "I was so young. New York was another world to a girl from Modrine, Indiana and I loved it and hated it and was scared to death every minute."

She took a sip of her tea. "When I got the chance to join a road company, I thought I was really on my way. Three weeks in Chicago, then a tour of the Midwest. I would get to play in Indianapolis and prove to everyone back home that I had made it." A smile flickered across her face and died. "How innocent I was."

"I met Nick the first night in Chicago. He came backstage. He was magnificent, gorgeous, dark and dangerous looking. It was just like a romance novel."

I blushed. Uncle Joe couldn't hold a candle to that.

"I married him before the company left Chicago."

"Three weeks?" Mom asked.

"Three weeks. Three incredible weeks of flowers, candy, gifts - a mink coat. I gave the coat back. He gave me a diamond bracelet. I refused to accept it. I think I must have driven him mad. He thought it was some kind of a game. It wasn't. I honestly didn't believe it was right to take expensive gifts from a man unless you were serious about getting married. That's what Mama taught me in Modrine."

We didn't answer. That's what Mom taught me, too.

"The wedding was simple, before a Justice of the Peace. I didn't know then that even though our marriage was completely legal, it was a joke to the Novaks. I was a Protestant, Nick a Catholic. The JP was not a priest, so it wasn't a real marriage to them. Just an excuse to get this dumb girl into bed." She paused and looked at me to see if I was shocked. Obviously she hadn't seen any movies lately or watched TV.

She took a deep breath. "We went off on a fabulous honeymoon in Miami."

Mom and I exchanged glances. They found Larry Novak's body in Miami.

"At first Nick was wonderful, loving, funny, so sweet. Then one night he came back to our hotel room furious. Some business thing had gone sour. He hit me."

She closed her eyes, remembering. "That was the beginning. After that first time, whenever he was angry, he'd slap me. Finally, he got so he'd slap me when he wasn't angry. Just for something to do. I told him I was leaving." She stopped.

Mom took her hand. "And..."

"And he threatened to kill me if I tried. I think he meant it."

I heard Havoc's nails click on the floor as he came in to join us. Jullian screamed and curled up in her chair.

"Sit, Havoc," Mom ordered. He sat. "He won't hurt you, Jillian. Really."

Jillian trembled so hard she shook the table.

Mom ordered Havoc out of the room. He stood to full dignity and walked into the other room to lie down in front of the cold fireplace.

Mom patted Jillian's hand. "He won't come near you. Do you want me to put him outside, or will you be all right with him in the next room?"

"I'm okay. Really. It's okay with him in there." But she was still shaking.

I didn't know what to do. "How about in your bedroom, Mom?"

She nodded. I pointed to the bedroom and said, "Havoc, go." He rose and went where I was pointing. A terrific dog.

That made it a little better. Mom and I looked at Jillian, but neither one of us asked her anything. After a long time she took a sip of her cold tea and looked straight at Mom. She raised her right arm above her head so we could see the underneath side with two long white scars running halfway down the inside of her arm. "I did try to leave him once. He set his Doberman on me."

We stared in horror at the scars. She dropped her arm. "He said no one would ever leave him. While I stood there bleeding, he said that no one would ever hurt his family and live, and he shot the dog right in front of me."

Mom and I both shuddered. Jillian looked at me. "I was a prisoner in that gaudy mansion on the Novak estate. I could only leave if one of Nick's men went with me. I had no friends. I was allowed to call my mother and father once a week on an extension phone, with Nick listening on the other line."

She lowered her head and rubbed the back of her neck with her right hand. Mom said gently, "Jillian, you don't have to tell us all this."

"Yes, I do. Otherwise you'll never understand why I want you to have the police here tonight and tomorrow. Nick's family is perfectly capable of stealing my son's body to be sure I never have anything to do with him, even in death."

She rubbed her neck again. "When I got pregnant Nick quit hitting me. His father said no man should strike a woman who carries his child. It was so strange. Nick's family didn't consider me his legitimate wife but my baby was a Novak. One of theirs. From the time he was born I was only allowed to see him for a few minutes each day. A cousin came in to take care of him.

"Nick's mother never spoke to me. She never used my name. 'That woman' is how she referred to me. I knew she would never help me take my son and escape."

"What did you do?" I had to ask.

"One evening when Larry was around seven months old, Nick's cousin brought Larry a kitten and Nick let me go into the nursery to watch the baby play with it. I was so excited. I thought maybe they would let me hold him for a few minutes if I didn't act too eager.

"He was sitting up, beginning to crawl. He was the most beautiful baby I've ever seen, dark hair and eyes like his father, but with my father's dimple in his chin." She sighed. "Nick set him down on the floor on a blanket and put the kitten down next to him. Larry grabbed it and the kitten scratched him. Before anyone could move Nick had grabbed the kitten and strangled it before our eyes. Larry was screaming. The cousin was crying. I was just numb. I reached for my baby and Nick's cousin grabbed him up and held him away from me. Nick pushed me out of the room. I still can hear him snarling at me, "Nothing hurts one of mine."

Mom rubbed her throat. I shuddered.

"That was when I knew I had to get out of there before I lost my mind. I was getting as crazy as they were. The next time one of Nick's men drove me downtown to Marshall Fields, I slipped away from him through a side door and took a city bus to a convent where one of Nick's sisters had been a novice. I had only been there once, but I remembered it as a safe place.

"Getting off the bus and going up to the gate were the most terrifying moments of my life. I was sure Nick was right behind me. The gate was locked. I rang the bell feeling like a target out in the open with all of Chicago watching me. It seemed like hours before a nun spoke to me from behind a grill. I think I was babbling by then. She let me in and took me to the Mother Superior.

"I had to tell her the truth or she would never have let me stay. I was so afraid because of the Novak's wealth and power. But more than that, one of those nuns out there in the convent may have been Nick's sister. I begged for sanctuary. Finally, the Mother Superior agreed, reluctantly. I was to sleep on the far side of the convent, away from the nuns. I couldn't go to mass with them, but I could go to the chapel and pray when no one was there. I was not to speak to any of the nuns, and none of them would speak to me. I could stay as long as I needed to, but I would have chores.

"That was when I told her I was pregnant. I remember how she sighed. 'And what do you want to do with the baby?' I didn't know. I was so terrified that Nick would find me that I couldn't think. I knew I couldn't involve my family. I couldn't go home. I had no friends in Chicago.

"I stayed in a small, plain room, very different from my bedroom in the mansion. It was wonderful. Quiet. Safe. Or at least I felt safe there. I could hear the nuns singing at mass, and sometimes I would see them gliding through the hallways, heads bowed so I couldn't see their faces, hands hidden in their sleeves. They still wore habits in those days, and that set them far apart from the ugliness of the rest of the world. I was so afraid that one of them might be Nick's sister that I didn't even try to get near any of them.

"When the time came for the baby to be born I felt as if I had been in the convent a lifetime. I knew I had to make a decision. If I left Chicago with Nick's child he would hunt me down in any corner of the earth I tried to hide in. Neither I nor the baby would ever be safe from him. I let the Mother Superior arrange an adoption to take place as soon as I delivered. I didn't want to see the baby, or even to know if it were a boy or a girl."

She stopped suddenly. Mom didn't say a word, and I didn't either. My throat hurt.

"The baby was a girl. It was a difficult delivery. They expected me to die. Maybe they hoped I would. I know I did. But I was tougher than I thought. Just before the family came to take my baby one of the nuns brought her to me and let me hold her. I knew I shouldn't take her, but I couldn't stop myself." Jillian's eyes were dark. "She was perfect, dark like Larry, beautiful. I called her Julia, but I'm sure the family who adopted her changed her name. Two weeks later I left the convent and went to California on a Greyhound Bus. I've never seen either one of my children since."

She turned away from us and swallowed her tears. "Now, with Larry's casket closed I won't even be able to say good-bye to him."

Mom and I sat silent. I looked at Jillian Montgomery, rich, slender, beautiful, with her real gold jewelry and a huge, glittering diamond ring and thought she must be the saddest person I had ever seen in my life.

"Jillian," Mom said, "I'm so sorry."

Jillian smiled and smoothed back her blonde-streaked hair with her left hand. The diamond caught the light and flashed its cold light at me. "Oh, that was a long time ago. I met Chris in

California. He was a good man, good to me. We never had any children. He died last year."

She seemed to reach inside somewhere and get strong. "But that's all in the past. It's now that has me worried. The Novaks are involved in every illegal activity you've ever hear of, drugs, prostitution, gambling, gun running. They're completely without mercy if anyone gets in their way, and just as completely without guilt. If they want Larry's body, they'll take it, unless we can stop them."

"I had another breather," I blurted out. I had almost forgotten the phone call.

Mom looked from me to Jillian. "Wait here," she said, and left to get Mike.

I didn't know what to say to Jillian Montgomery. Hey, I'm sorry you married the Mob. Gee, too bad about the scars on your arm, and on your soul. Too bad you had to pay such a big price for a mistake you made when you were eighteen. I felt a chill. In two years I'd be eighteen. I could ruin my whole life. I wanted to jump up and call Molly and tell her about Nick Novak. Warn her again about Trevor Lewis. Maybe, I thought, I could become a nun if you don't have to be Catholic.

"Larry's father," I said suddenly, "is he dead?"

"He was murdered." She paused for a moment trying to decide whether to tell me the rest of it. "He was gunned down coming out of a restaurant with Paulie and Sammy, his brother. Paulie used to be my bodyguard."

"Was he the one you escaped from?"

She closed her eyes. "No. That was Steve. He disappeared about the same time I did." She opened her eyes and looked at me. "I'm sure they killed him for letting me get away."

"My biological grandfather was killed in a fight in a tavern before Mom was born." I don't know why I told her that. "I never told anyone before. It's a secret. Matt and I overheard Gran talking about it when we were little kids."

Jillian reached across the table and took my hand. Usually I don't like to have anyone touch me, but right then it was all right.

Mom and Mike came in and sat down. Cold tea skimmed over in the cups while the bread on my peanut butter and sweet pickle sandwich dried out.

"Maggie tells me you think we need to have police protection tonight and tomorrow."

"Yes."

"I'll call the sheriff right now. Okay?"

She shook her head. "No. Don't call from here. Your phone is probably tapped. In fact, the house may be bugged, too. That's the way they operate."

Mike considered. "The phone maybe, but not the house. No one has been in the quarters. When we've been gone Havoc has been here."

I thought about when Jed got out and someone poisoned Havoc. Someone had been in the funeral home then. And all night on Friday. I kept quiet.

She nodded. "Do you have another phone?"

Mom stood. "I'll get my cell phone out of the van."

While she was gone Jillian smiled weakly at Mike. "Thank you for taking this seriously. I'm sure it sounds like a bad TV movie."

Mom handed Mike the phone. He dialed the sheriff's office. "Hey, Mike here. Is Harold busy?"

Hey? I couldn't believe I heard him say that.

"Harold. Mike here. It was great having you stay with us last night. How would you like a repeat? Maybe Maggie could make another pineapple upside down cake. What do you think? Great."

What a rotten actor! He couldn't fool Havoc with that voice, let alone a real professional crook. He sounded like a bad combination of British and Southern, kind of Bubba and Patrick Stewart from Star Trek. We were a bunch of amateurs playing a game we didn't understand and the other guys were winning.

Chapter Twenty Nine

"They're all dead!" Matt came into the kitchen, ran into the corner of the cabinet and then leaned on the counter.

Mom and Mike stood quickly. "Who?" they both said at once.

"The angel fish. I was checking the connecting door upstairs and thought I'd look around. They're all dead."

Mike's face turned gray. "You shouldn't have gone into the funeral home by yourself, Matt."

Matt nodded. He looked a little wild eyed.

We went upstairs. All the beautiful fish floated on top of the water in their 20-gallon tank, the air filter still pumping away. An empty bottle of window cleaner sat next to the tank as if to say, This is how I did it...easily, and with something you never feared.

Mike acted calm, but he kept jingling the change in his pants pocket and tugging on his tie. He fed the fish personally every day and Gabriel used to come right to the top of the water like he knew Mike. I'm not big on fish, but those were pretty neat, and Mike thought they were soothing to watch. "Something alive for families to see in the face of death." Now they were dead, too.

Jillian leaned against the wall, as pale as Matt. "He's killed one more thing to punish me." I think she meant Nick, but not really Nick, because he was already dead. Someone living killed the fish.

When Harold came, Mike took him up to see the tank. "Don't take them out until I get a photographer here. You didn't touch the window cleaner bottle, did you? I doubt if we'll find any prints, but we'll check it."

If good old Harold was all business with the fish, he turned into a creepy crawly with Jillian, calling her "Ms. Montgomery" every chance he had, hanging on every word like a guy with a major crush. I wanted to barf.

I folded when he said, "Ms. Montgomery, I don't want you to worry about anything. I'll be staying the night here, with my brown and tan parked right out there under the overhang so those criminals know this place is protected."

Havoc went upstairs with me and jumped to the foot of my bed when I crawled in. I wasn't sure why he decided I deserved the honor, but I was glad to have him.

I heard Jillian leave around midnight I felt exhausted, but I couldn't go to sleep. I wondered how Mr. Modrine was. I didn't know who won the Indianapolis 500. I missed Molly. I wondered how it would feel to have to run away and leave your little boy and then give away your baby girl. I think that's when I fell asleep.

I remember every detail about the dream. I was walking around inside the funeral home in the dark with Willy and Havoc. I turned around to talk to them, but they were gone and Matt was there. I asked him where the casket was and he said in a strange soft voice, "In the basement."

We started toward the basement, but then we were in the formal chapel that Mike added to the funeral home when he bought it from Claude Ellis. The pep band from school stood around the outside of the room and strangers filled all the seats. They had eyes like cats, as if they knew secrets.

I walked to the casket and opened it and looked inside. I saw hundreds of guns, but no body. I turned to tell Jillian Montgomery that there was no body in the casket, but the chapel was empty. Walking in the door and coming toward me was the man who signed the register Ross Geller, carrying a kitten in one hand and a big gun that I knew as an AK-47, although I've never seen one in my life. He looked tall, dark and handsome, and very dangerous. He kept walking toward me, smiling, and said, "The living are more dangerous than the dead, little girl." Then he kissed me. I screamed.

Havoc was licking my face. I sat straight up, shaking all over. 3:15 glowed on the clock. The maple tapped, tapped on my window. The security light made the window seats shine like cloth of silver. I got up and walked around the room. Havoc walked with me. I reached down and patted his head. "You're a good dog."

He leaned against me, as if he agreed. I turned on the floor lamp and moved it from the chair to next to the bed. Mom gave it to me when we first moved in because she's a reader, too. I reached for the book I left there two days, a hundred years ago. Stephen King. No way. Not tonight.

I scooted under the covers and reached for the light. Havoc jumped back up on the bed. "I love you, dog." His tail thumped against the covers.

When I woke, daylight streamed in the windows. 10:45. Oh, no. Fifteen minutes to Larry Novak's funeral. Everyone would be in the chapel by now. I needed a chance to slip in and open the casket to see what was really in there. What if it was full of guns, like in my dream? What if there was no body at all? Any dream that real had to be true. How could I prove it?

Matt must have let Havoc out. I put on my black jeans, my black Phantom of the Opera sweatshirt and my black running shoes. Ninja Leigh, Girl Detective, yellow belt in karate, will solve this case. Stupid.

I went downstairs. No one. Havoc paced the yard, guarding the house. Mom and Matt must be watching the guests while Mike worked the door. I went into the garage and sure enough, the coach was parked under the overhang ready for the casket to be loaded and taken to the cemetery.

I looked over at Roselawn, already full of cars. Bright sun, cool air, a beautiful Memorial Day. Modrine used to have a parade. Now all the people who used to go to the parade went to the cemetery instead.

Back in the garage I tried the prep room door. Unlocked. I slipped through to the side door of the formal chapel and opened the door a crack so I could see what was going on.

The casket, a 48 ounce bronze, the most expensive one Ellis and Pearson carries, sat on the bier in front of the pulpit with a big spray of red roses on it. Other baskets of flowers, probably from Mrs. Hamilton's society friends, sat on either side. Jillian and her mother sat on the front row, both very straight and dignified in black. Jillian's uncle, Vernon Hamilton, president of the bank, Power Man, sat between his sister-in-law and his wife Evelyn, Queen of the Modrine Country Club. Neither of them looked particularly grief stricken.

Behind the Hamiltons sat three strangers, Geller and two other hoods. Geller stared at the back of Jillian's head as if he wanted to rip it off and throw it through the stained glass window. I shuddered a little and wondered why such a hateful look didn't burn a hole in the back of her head. I bet he was one of those Chicago Novaks she worried about.

I recognized most of the people in the crowded chapel, except for the three in the second row and a couple of average-looking guys in business suits at the back who didn't look suspicious. Harold, wearing his sheriff's uniform, stood by the entry doors, hand close to his pistol. Sic'em, Barney.

When the organ music stopped, the new Methodist minister rose to speak. Young Reverend Esterhouse didn't have a clue about Larry Novak, but he knew he'd better not offend the Hamiltons. He kept saying "the bereaved" and "the deceased" and didn't tell any personal anecdotes about "the deceased" because no one knew any except Jillian, and the strangled kitten story probably wouldn't be a good one to tell. Jillian couldn't seem to quit crying, but nobody else shed a tear.

While Kevin escorted people out to their cars for the drive to the cemetery, Mike and Dwight loaded the casket into the coach.

I shut the door, and ran back through the prep room, through the garage, stopping long enough to pick up a casket crank key on the table in the prep room. The crack is used to raise and lower the lining of the casket and the key part locks the ends. I would need it to open the casket and look for the guns.

Mike always followed the same routine: he started the coach, then went back into the chapel to make sure everything was in order before leaving for the cemetery. Meanwhile, Kevin loaded the flowers to take to the cemetery where they would be left on the grave, setting aside the potted plants to take to the family later. Dwight went down the line of cars telling people to turn on their headlights. He made sure all the funeral flags were in place on the front fenders. Then Dwight got into the family car behind the coach. Mike came out and got into the coach and they left for the cemetery.

I watched for my chance. During the time that Mike got out of the coach to go back into the funeral home, I had to get into the back of the coach and open the casket. When they saw the guns they would know why the Mob wanted to steal the casket. They didn't want poor old Larry Novak's body, they wanted the guns. They probably dumped him somewhere in Miami.

As soon as Mike started the engine, turned on the lights and got out, I ran to the side door of the silver coach. The chapel door shut behind Mike at the same time that I slipped into the coach, crawled in next to the casket and closed the door tightly behind me. I made sure the plastic divider was closed between me and the front seat, and straightened the curtains. That made it pretty dark, but I could see well enough to find the lock.

Slipping the spray of red roses off the top of the casket, I laid it carefully on the floor behind me so it wouldn't be damaged. I had to hurry. Roselawn was a short drive. The key clicked in the lock as I turned it. Just a couple of inches should be enough to see the guns. I knew there was no lifeless corpse in the casket. It was full of guns.

The heavy lid wouldn't budge. I tugged and tugged, but I couldn't pry it open. I tried to lie down and push on the lid with my feet, but couldn't get situated right.This should have been so simple.

As soon as Mike got in the coach to drive to the cemetery, I would tell him. He could go ahead with the internment at the mausoleum, and then go back with the police after the family left. That was a better plan anyway. Maybe if I hadn't overslept I might have thought of it sooner.

Just then the driver's door opened and Mike got in. I reached for the divider to tell him what I was doing when the coach took off like a scalded cat and threw me back into the roses. What!? No one ever drives a coach fast when there is a body in the back.

We careened around a corner, and I bounced sideways against the casket. I pulled myself up to reach for the divider again and ask Mike if he had lost his mind when we skidded around another corner. Thank God the casket was wedged in by the casket stops or I would have been crushed. I didn't need to pull the curtains aside to know that Mike wasn't driving the coach, not in a million years.

We accelerated and I flew back into the roses again. Those flowers were history. We must have been going seventy at least. At this rate we would soon be doing ninety, maybe faster. A wreck at this speed and there would really be a dead body in the back. Mine.

I crawled out of the roses and pulled the curtain aside a fraction of an inch to peek at the driver. I let the curtain drop with my stomach. Of course. I knew it even before I looked that it would be Geller with his crazy, hate-filled eyes, driving like a bat out of hell. I was trapped in a run-away coach with a gun-running maniac.

Hanging on to the side and to the casket handles to give me some stability, I crawled over the top of the casket so I wouldn't be in the flowers any more. On the other side I scooted to the back of the coach and pulled the curtain aside. There, screaming along behind us was the funeral cortege, headlights shining in the sun. Dwight, hands clenched on the wheel of the Cadillac family car, stayed right with us. The little Ellis and Pearson flag on the fender flew straight back like a wind sock in a hurricane. I waved at him.

I couldn't hear him, but even a bad lip reader could see him saying, "Oh, my God." I kept waving. Jillian leaned up next to him from the back seat and waved back. I could see her talking to Dwight.

Behind him were three of four other cars, still following at this speed, lights shining, flags flapping as we raced down the interstate. The other cars that lined up at the funeral home must have felt they couldn't make the qualification run and dropped out of the race.

If what the mob wants is the casket maybe I could take out the casket stop from the back, open the doors and roll it out. Then Geller would have to stop if he wanted his guns. I reached over to twist up the tightening screw so I could pull up the eight-inch square casket stop. It was actually wiggling loose when the thought hit me—Jillian didn't know about my dream, or about the guns. She still thought her son was in the casket. If I pushed it out the back door of the coach she would think her son's body was being desecrated. Bad. Besides, what if the casket hit the family car and caused a wreck? Very bad idea. I tightened the screw back down.

I could take the casket crank key out of my pocket, open the divider and stick the key in good old Geller's back and tell him it was a gun. Then I'd make him pull over. Sure. As if he'd believe a weak little soprano was holding a gun on him.

We were off the interstate on a rough road. We accelerated up a hill and I slammed into the back doors. He might not have to kill me when we stopped. At this rate the drive would beat me to death.

I couldn't believe he was stupid enough to steal a coach at the funeral. How did he think he could get away with it? Where were we going? The abandoned air strip? If his gang was waiting somewhere for us, they would see me as soon as they opened the door. My stomach did a triple and landed in my shoes.

That was when I heard the sirens, distant, but clear. Harold? With my luck it would be an ambulance on the way to a wreck. Maybe someone saw a run-away funeral procession and drove into a ditch. I lay on the floor next to the casket full of guns and held onto the handles for dear life.

The sirens grew louder. The coach swung from side to side, accelerating until I could hear the engine strain. If we were on the country road that led to the old airport that would explain the potholes and pits we kept hitting.

I rolled over and tried to get on my knees. I pulled the curtain aside and looked behind us. Only Dwight in the family car had made it this far. He hunched over the wheel, intense with concentration, looking like A. J. Foyt, out of retirement. Jillian had crawled over the seat and perched next to him, bouncing up and down as they navigated the road. She waved at me. I waved back. I wanted to say, "Your son isn't in here," but there was no way.

The sirens grew louder. More than one. I could see flashing red lights behind Dwight. He eased over to the edge of the road to let an Indiana State Police cruiser come up behind the coach. The trooper didn't look like he wanted to wave at me.

We swerved again and I slammed against the wall hard. Everything went black for a few seconds. Wow. I decided to lie down again.

The sirens screamed. We swerved hard as the maniac slammed on his brakes and tried to keep the coach under control. The sudden braking pitched me forward and my feet were up against the front seat. I kept my knees bent to absorb some of the shock and I prayed. It seemed like a good time to include God in the mess I was in.

A final jolt and the coach stopped. We tilted at a funny angle. My feet, pressed against the back of the front seat, were lower than my head. Maybe we were in a ditch. I decided to lie very still and hope Geller didn't decide to get a gun out of the casket to try to hold off the cops. Shoot out in Indiana.

I heard a loud speaker voice say, "Get out of the hearse with your hands over your head." Nothing happened. The door didn't open. No sound from the front seat. Maybe the maniac had been hurt when we landed wherever we were.

The plexiglass window on the passenger side slid back and a hand pulled the curtain to one side. I held my breath and tried to be invisible. Was he going to try to climb through the window to the back to try to get out through the rear doors? I didn't think he could do it, not through an opening too small for Matt and almost too small for me. Please don't let him find an uninvited guest next to the casket he had tried to steal.

"Come out of the hearse with your hands up. We have all exits covered. Surrender now, or we'll take you out." Take you out—like blow you away? Help you climb out? Riddle the coach with machine gun fire like in the movies?

I held my breath and closed my eyes. Then I heard the best sound in the world, the door to the coach opening.

"Throw out your gun," the voice on the loud speaker ordered.

Severe cursing from the front seat. He must have thrown out the gun because the next thing I heard was, "Slide out of the hearse with your hands up."

I heard movement, grunting, then silence. I lay still for long moments, wondering where he was. Then the back doors flew open and Dwight was there reaching for me. He sounded frantic, "Leigh. Leigh. Are you all right?"

I looked back over my head and grinned. A pretty sickly grin, but the best I could do. "Bumped a little, but I think I'm okay." I rolled over on my stomach and crawled up toward the back doors. Dwight took my hands and pulled me to him. I could see the red lights flashing all around us from six or seven police cars.

I scrambled out and Dwight hugged me so hard it nearly smothered me. "You really had us worried, kid. What were you doing in the coach?"

"It's a long story."

Jillian scrambled down the hill to us and grabbed me when Dwight let me go. I must have scared them all.

We moved together toward the police cars at the top of the ditch. My legs hurt and my head ached. I hung onto Dwight. When we reached level ground I could see the man who called himself Geller, with his hands cuffed behind him and a state trooper holding onto him. About then Harold ran up, out of breath. "I had to park clear back there," he panted, pointing past the trees.

He looked at me in amazement and shook his head. "Leigh! What are you doing here?"

Dwight grinned. "She was joy riding."

Harold looked confused.

Just then Jillian gasped and staggered against us. Dwight let go of me and grabbed her. The color left her face so that her eyes looked like dark moons. I grabbed her other arm before she passed out. She leaned on me, limp as spaghetti, staring ahead at something that terrified her. Then I saw where she was looking. Her eyes locked on Geller and he glared at her with the same hate-filled expression I saw in the chapel.

She shook us off and walked unsteadily over to where three more troopers had gathered. She walked through them even though one of them tried to hold her back. I stuck right behind her. "Who are you?" she whispered, looking straight at Geller.

His smile had all the warmth of a piranha. "You don't know me? I'm Lorenzo Novak."

She staggered again. A trooper caught her. "Dear God," she whispered, "you're Larry."

He seemed to bow slightly, mockingly. "And you, of course, are my faithless whore of a mother."

She slid to the ground like a black bag of laundry, a body without bones. I never saw anyone faint before. The largest trooper picked her up as if she were a baby.

A police officer pushed Larry Novak's head down so he could get into the back seat of the cruiser. I saw his black eyes for a second before they closed the door.

"Let's get out of here," Dwight said. "Your folks will be crazy."

"Wait. Wait!" I twisted away from him. "Listen, if this is Larry Novak, what do you suppose is in the casket? He's a gun runner or something. He's hiding something in the casket." My voice must have gotten shrill because Dwight grabbed my arm.

"Don't worry, Miss," one of the officers said, "we'll check it out."

Dwight led me to the empty family car. I saw Gertrude Hamilton in one of the cruisers. Jillian's head was on her shoulder. Dwight put me in the front seat. "Stay here. I've got to use the radio in Harold's car to try to rent a coach. We've got another funeral this afternoon at two. Will you be okay till I get back?"

I nodded and leaned back against the seat. I closed my eyes. Another funeral. Kippy's mother would be buried this afternoon, and she was really dead, like all the other people Mike takes care of. Once they closed the casket, Kippy would never see her mother's face again. Tears started to run down my cheeks. I hated Larry Novak. He and his evil friends had used a casket to transport something illegal, probably guns, and then he had driven the coach like a madman down the interstate. No dignity for death, nothing solemn.

I thought of Jillian and the way he looked at her. His own mother. Why did he hate her so much? Because she ruined the Mob's operation by having the casket sent to Modrine? Because she left him and ran away from his father? Who knows what the Novaks told him about her. Now they would have a trial and she would have to be there. I cried harder.

Dwight crawled into the car. "Let's go home, kid. Mrs. Hamilton is going to ride to the hospital with Mrs. Montgomery."

"Is she okay?"

"Routine check. Just to be sure. Her mother wanted to go along."

I nodded. "Let's go home."

CHAPTER THIRTY

Back at the funeral home things looked normal out front, but in back we found a state police cruiser and next to it a strange black car. Inside Mom, Mike and Matt waited for us with a state trooper and two strangers I recognized from the funeral. Mom flew across the room and grabbed me. "Leigh! Where on earth have you been? We've been nearly crazy worrying about you.!"

Her red face and swollen eyes laid a guilt trip on me. I hugged her hard so she would know I was okay.

Matt stood behind her with a look on his face that said he had a hundred questions, at least. I tried to signal to him that we'd talk later. He seemed to understand, because he gave me a little grin and stepped back a little.

Mike hadn't gotten up from the table when we came in. He held an ice pack to his head and gave me a funny, half-sick grin.

"What happened to Mike?" I asked.

He looked up at me with a weak smile. "Someone decided I'd make a good broom."

"What?"

The stranger explained. "He was hit on the head and dragged into the broom closet in the garage right before the hearse was stolen."

"The coach," I said automatically.

He raised his eyebrows in a question. I shook my head. "We call it a coach, not a hearse."

The man cleared his throat uneasily. He must have thought I was nuts.

"Did you catch the others? The ones who were helping Jillian's son?" I asked.

Mom gasped. Matt whistled softly. Mike just sat looking stunned.

The stranger said, "We have two men in custody, but it may be hard to prove anything since there are no witnesses."

I looked at his level gray eyes. "Do you think they're the guys who poisoned our dog and our fish and beat up on Mr. Modrine."

"It's quite likely, but again..." he paused.

"There are no witnesses," Matt finished. He spread the sarcasm thick as peanut butter.

"Does that mean they're going to get away with it?" The anger built inside me like steam in a tea kettle. "Those guys tormented us for days. They've hurt people and scared people and let our bird loose. What do you mean 'there are no witnesses'? I'm a witness."

"Innocent until proven guilty," Matt said. From the tone of his voice I guessed they must have gone over this before I came in, probably several times.

I plopped down on one of the empty kitchen chairs. Mom stood behind me with her hands on my shoulders, hanging onto me so I wouldn't get away again. "This really stinks."

The other man cleared his throat. They did that a lot. Probably embarrassed. "There are some other charges we can bring against them, however."

"Like what?" I felt belligerent and nasty. My legs and back hurt and my head ached.

He smiled and looked mysterious. Creep.

"Like maybe transporting illegal weapons across the state line? I know there was something in that casket besides a body. That's why I got in the coach to try to open the casket to find out. I dreamed they were smuggling guns."

I narrowed my eyes and looked at the two strangers. "You're federal agents of some kind, aren't you?"

Neither one answered. Mike said, "Yes, they are."

"It wasn't guns, was it? I bet it was drugs." I glared at the shorter agent, who stood silently behind Mike.

He looked at his partner, sighed and said, "That's right. We've been on to them for months, but we needed to intercept a shipment and catch them with it. The small fry are already in the net. Novak was the one we wanted."

Mom pressed her hands down on my shoulders, making sure I didn't get away again. "What about Larry Novak's body?" she asked.

I twisted around to look at her. "His body is in custody, walking around and talking. He wasn't dead at all." I met Matt's eyes. "He's Ross Geller."

The agent who hadn't talked before said, "From television?"

Matt said, "I made him sign the guest register at Harry Friedman's funeral and he signed it Ross Geller. Big joke."

The two men nodded. I thought we should all nod, except my head hurt too much. Mike looked like his hurt worse than mine.

"You look beat right now, so we can wait to ask you a few questions. We'll need statements from all of you, and you'll need to identify the men you've seen here in the funeral home."

Mike moved the ice pack a little. "They're on video tape."

The agents snapped to attention. The second one said, "What video tape?"

Mike groaned a little. "We have video camera on the doors. After the trouble started we hooked up the VCR and started taping all the people who've come into the funeral home during the past three days."

For the first time the two agents smiled. They looked almost human. "That's excellent. We'll need to take those tapes."

Mom looked hesitant. The state trooper spoke for the first time. "Do you have a way to make copies, Mrs. Pearson?"

Mom nodded.

"Let's do that right now, and then these agents can take the originals."

Mom still hesitated.

"They'll sign for them. It'll be okay."

With a little shrug she led them out of the kitchen into the chapel and to the office in the front of the building.

Mike looked at his watch. I checked mine. Still ticking. Not bad. 11:55 A.M. Could it have been less than an hour since I crawled into the coach?

"Matt, you're going to have to work the door with Dwight for Estelle Brown's funeral. Kevin will help get everything ready. I think I need to lie down. Do you think you can do it?"

Matt drew himself up. "I think I can handle it."

Maybe now he would forgive me for being the one in the coach with Larry Novak, dead man driving.

Dwight smiled at Mike. "Don't worry, buddy," he said. "Matt and Kevin and I can handle things. We don't need you."

I recognized the man-to-man insulting that meant they really liked each other. I will never understand men.

Dwight started to go into the funeral home, stopped and turned back to Mike. "When that kid pulled back the curtain on the coach and I saw her face, well, believe me, that was one of life's weirdest moments. Jillian Montgomery climbed right over the seat and kept yelling at me, 'Don't let them get away. Don't let them get away.' I swear, when she saw Leigh she went radical on me. It was one wild ride."

Mike turned cautiously to look at me, his eyes like black holes. "What were you trying to do in there?"

"I was going to open the casket to see if there were guns in it. But I couldn't get it open. It was a stupid idea," I finished lamely.

He tried to smile. "Did you forget there was a Ziegler Box in the casket? Even if you had opened the lid, you wouldn't have found anything."

I closed my eyes. "Oh, no. I completely forgot about the Ziegler."

"It's okay, Leigh. You were very brave."

I didn't feel brave. I felt stupid and tired and every bone and muscle in my body hurt. I could feel the tears burn in my throat. "I wasn't brave, Mike, I was lucky."

Chapter Thirty One

We all testified at the trial: Mom, Mike, Matt, Dwight, Harold and I. It took a long time to get through because of all the delays. The big-time Chicago attorneys kept getting continuances. They got a change of venue to another county, but it didn't help much, just took more time.

The newspapers covered the trial like a heavy rain. Television reporters were like fleas all over everyone. The prosecutor took us through back doors and down guarded halls to testify. The excitement was pretty neat at first, but it got old fast.

A couple of families changed the pre-arrangements for funerals that they had made and paid for a long time ago. Then, after a couple of months, they changed them back. Mike said we lost a few calls, but not many.

The prosecutor charged Larry Novak with criminal confinement while carrying a weapon, resisting arrest, auto theft, kidnapping in the commission of a felony, possession of a controlled substance with intent to deliver, and a couple of other things I've forgotten. I had to spend a lot of time in a dumpy room with Matt and Mike and Mom and Dwight because we couldn't be in the court room during the trial. "Separation of witnesses," they call it. Boring is what I call it. Lucky for me I like to read.

Finally, Larry Novak was sentenced to eighty-five years in prison. He was taken to Plainfield to the Reception and Diagnostic Center, and the Department of Corrections placed him in maximum security in the prison at Pendleton. The other two were tried in Indiana first, then scheduled to be extradited to Florida for crimes committed there. A nice bunch of crooks.

During the trial it came out that the drug ring they were part of was using Miami as a home base, with Chicago as the

Midwest distribution center for cities like St. Louis, Louisville, Indianapolis, Nashville, Columbus, Detroit, Minneapolis and Milwaukee. The cocaine in the Ziegler had a street value in the millions. They used a funeral home in Miami, a casket shipping company and dummy funeral homes in the cities they shipped to. It was a slick operation, busted by a small town funeral director and a grieving mother.

Mike kept saying things like, "How could they? How dare they do something like this? It makes all funeral homes look bad. People will think we're all drug dealers." Mom tried to reason with him. It didn't help much.

The television cameras loved filming Jillian Montgomery at the trial every day, watching her watch her son, who ignored her completely and refused to see her.

Mom called her a couple of times, and they went out for lunch, but Mom never said what they talked about. Jillian's still in Modrine, living with her mother.

Mike won the primary nomination for coroner. Mom wasn't sure she wanted him to win. I didn't care. I figured he'd be good at it.

I made up with Molly before she broke up with Trevor, the Creep. I'm glad it worked out that way because I was there for her when he dumped her to go back to Tiffany Taggart. We started working at the Sweet Shoppe and I liked having my own money. I intended to save up to buy my own car. I wanted one painted the same color all over, with windshield wipers that work.

Things got back to normal, I guess. But, sometimes, when it storms, or if things have gone wrong all day, I dream I'm in the back of the coach, speeding down the interstate with Larry Novak laughing, laughing in the front seat, and the lid of the casket slowly opening. That's when I wake up and remember that the living are more dangerous than the dead.